Emma Emmets
PLAYGROUND MATCHMAKER

Emma Emmets
PLAYGROUND MATCHMAKER

Julia DeVillers

razor
bill

AN IMPRINT OF PENGUIN GROUP (USA) INC.

Published by the Penguin Group

Penguin Group (USA) Inc.

375 Hudson Street, New York, New York 10014, USA

Penguin Group (Canada), 90 Eglinton Avenue East, Suite 700, Toronto, Ontario M4P 2Y3, Canada (a division of Pearson Penguin Canada Inc.); Penguin Books Ltd, 80 Strand, London WC2R 0RL, England; Penguin Ireland, 25 St Stephen's Green, Dublin 2, Ireland (a division of Penguin Books Ltd); Penguin Group (Australia), 707 Collins St., Melbourne, Victoria 3008, Australia (a division of Pearson Australia Group Pty Ltd); Penguin Books India Pvt Ltd, 11 Community Centre, Panchsheel Park, New Delhi–110 017, India; Penguin Group (NZ), 67 Apollo Drive, Rosedale, Auckland 0632, New Zealand (a division of Pearson New Zealand Ltd); Penguin Books, Rosebank Office Park, 181 Jan Smuts Avenue, Parktown North 2193, South Africa; Penguin China, B7 Jaiming Center, 27 East Third Ring Road North, Chaoyang District, Beijing 100020, China

Penguin Books Ltd, Registered Offices: 80 Strand, London WC2R 0RL, England

ISBN: 978-1-59514-661-8

Published simultaneously in Canada

This book is set in Bell.

LIBRARY OF CONGRESS CATALOGING-IN-PUBLICATION DATA
is available

Printed in the United States of America

10   9   8   7   6   5   4   3   2   1

PUBLISHER'S NOTE: This is a work of fiction. Names, characters, places, and incidents either are the product of the author's imagination or are used fictitiously, and any resemblance to actual persons, living or dead, businesses, companies, events, or locales is entirely coincidental.

To Jocelyn Davies, Literary Matchmaker

CHAPTER ♥ 1

Being a fourth grader definitely felt different, Emma decided as she walked along the sidewalk toward the elementary school. She felt older. More mature. For the first time, her parents had finally agreed to let her walk the two blocks to school without them. Emma had left the house super early to avoid them changing their minds at the last minute. (Even though they stood on the front steps and watched until she reached the corner with the Crossing Guard Lady, it definitely still counted as walking by herself. Definitely.)

"Happy first day of school! You're bright and early," the Crossing Guard Lady said as Emma reached the crosswalk.

"Happy first day!" Emma replied. "And yup, I am."

"You're even earlier than certain middle schoolers who are almost late to school," Crossing Guard Lady said loudly, as some sixth-grade boys from Emma's street trudged up behind them. The middle school, which was a few blocks farther, started earlier.

Crossing Guard Lady waved her GO sign, and they crossed the street.

"You guys better hurry," Emma pointed out.

"Oh look, it's a little baby elementary-school kid," one boy snarked. "Did you escape from your playpen? Where's your binky, elementary school baby?"

"At least elementary school babies have recess." Emma grinned as they stepped onto the sidewalk. "Recess on the BRAND NEW PLAYGROUND!"

They all stopped and stared. There in front of them, just past the sidewalk and the new white picket fence, in all its gloriousness, was the Brand! New! Playground! Over the summer, the old blah boring playground had been hauled away and a new one had risen in its place.

There was a jungle gym shaped like a pirate ship with a bridge and three curvy slides coming out of it: blue, yellow, and red. There were rows of swings, high monkey bars, a teeter-totter, a new basketball court, and a zip line!

The middle schoolers' faces fell as they witnessed the glory of the spectacular new playground.

"You guys only had three old swings and a metal slide and that gross old sandbox," Emma rubbed in. "Too bad, so sad."

Emma could hear the boys grumbling about the injustice as they continued on down the sidewalk toward the middle school a few blocks away.

Heh.

Emma walked up to the fence and peered in.

Brand new playground. Brand new school year. It all held so much promise. Emma was hoping fourth grade would be The Year. The Year of What, she didn't exactly know. But something. Something special and exciting.

Sure, third grade had been pretty good. But she'd had a couple of moments she'd prefer to forget. Let's just say her nickname had been EMbarrassing.

Emma was hoping that this year she would make a name for herself—but not a nickname.

Emma suddenly felt a little nervous. She checked to make sure she still looked okay in her silver shirt with sparkling sequins, black leggings, and silver ballet flats. She smoothed down her medium-length brown hair that swished against her shoulders. She double-checked her lucky bracelets:

* Braided brown leather bracelet

* Green-and-pink friendship bracelet she'd made at day camp (kind of scraggly)

* I ♡ Jake LaDrake rubber bracelet that came free with her Jake LaDrake singing toothbrush that played his hit song "You're My Perfect Match" while Emma brushed her teeth

Emma smiled. Just thinking about Jake LaDrake made her feel better. Jake, the teen singing sensation, oh-so-cute with his blond ruffly hair and his deep green eyes . . .

Emma knew that Jake would understand her nervousness. She had read in her Jake LaDrake special collector's edition magazine that Jake got nervous sometimes before his concerts, because he didn't want to let down his fans. That would be a lot of pressure.

A whole lot of pressure. Like starting your first day of fourth grade. Everyone had told her that fourth grade was when school gets harder. More tests. More drama. Teachers saying you weren't little kids anymore and you had to take more responsibility. Eeps!

"Great playground, isn't it?"

Emma jumped, startled. She turned to see Crossing Guard Lady standing behind her, smiling.

"Why don't you try it out?"

"Now?" Emma asked. "Really?"

"Why not?" Crossing Guard Lady said.

She pushed open the gate and held up her sign: GO.

Emma ran inside! She was the only person on the new playground.

It was like she owned it.

It was like Emma's EMpire.

Soon the school day would begin and the playground would be packed with kids crowding, waiting in lines, knocking each other out of the way. But for a little while, it would be like her very own.

Buzz!

Emma heard a buzzing noise coming from her backpack. She pulled out her cell phone and checked the text message that had popped up from her dad.

Yes, Emma had gotten her very own new cell phone, with a black-and-white cover shaped like a penguin, for her birthday a few weeks ago! She loved it! Emma answered her dad's text to let him know that yes, she was fine ☺. Then Emma texted one other person, her best friend, Claire, before slipping her phone back into the backpack.

And then it was time.

CHAPTER 2

Obviously, the first stop would be the zip line.

Emma ran over and grabbed the zip line handle with both hands. She gave herself a small push, but it left her moving only a few inches, dangling. Heh. Awkward. Emma was glad there was no one around to see her.

Emma pulled the zip line back and this time gave herself a serious push: *Zoom!* Emma was launched! She grinned as she went zipping, practically flying across the playground! And then—

Bap! She hit the end of the zip line *hard*, and vibrations shook through her whole body. *Sproing!* She dropped to the ground and fell over, flat on her face.

"Emma! Emma, are you okay?"

Emma looked up to see Claire leaning over her. Her bright blue eyes looked worried.

"That"—Emma spat-coughed a piece of woodchip mulch—"was awesome. Here's some advice, though: Keep your mouth closed when you zip."

"I can't believe we have the whole playground to ourselves," Claire said, looking around in disbelief.

Emma stood up and waved in the direction of Claire's mother's shiny white minivan, where Claire's mom was (as usual) hovering around the edges of her life.

"My mom wanted to know if we're allowed to be out here with no monitors or teachers," Claire asked.

"Yup," Emma said cheerfully. "The crossing guard is right there. She knows we're mature fourth graders who can be trusted on the playground. We can do anything we want!"

Claire's cell phone buzzed.

"My mom says not to get my outfit messy." Claire was wearing a light blue shirt, a light blue and white pin-striped skort, and white ballet flats. She had a light blue bow attached to her wavy blond hair.

"Then we can do anything except the zip line," Emma amended.

"Do you want to play basketball?" Claire asked. Claire loved basketball. Emma not so much. Emma slid her tongue over the gap where a wayward basketball had knocked out her tooth a few days ago at Happy Frogs Day Camp & Day Care. She shuddered, remembering how one of the boys had found it and refused to give it back. Seriously, Emma didn't think *finders keepers* counted with someone's personal teeth, but she'd been bleeding too hard to fight for it.

"Let's swing!" Emma said. Emma ran to a swing, and Claire gave her a push before hopping onto the next one over. Emma leaned back and pumped. At recess, there was a two-minute rule for the swings so everyone could have a turn, but right now, she could swing forever. Or at least until the early bell rang.

"Fourth grade is going to be different," Emma said as she whizzed past Claire. "I can feel it."

"Different good or different bad?" Claire asked. She tilted back to pump her legs, her long blond hair flying behind her. "Oh no, it's going to be bad, isn't it?"

"Claire, don't be negative. It's going to be *good* different," Emma said emphatically. "We're going to have a *good* year. We're going to *own* fourth grade."

Emma made a flying leap off the swing and ran over to the new jungle gym. She walked across the bridge and climbed the platform steps to the very top, where a black telescope perched on its ledge.

Emma put her eye up to the telescope. Ah! She could see everything. The entire playground and the back of her school. She could see the crossing guard at the corner and Claire's mother's minivan. Hey, she could see the roof of her own house!

Then she spotted a flash of orangey-yellow blur in the distance. The buses were coming! Emma adjusted the telescope until she had a clear view and watched as the buses pulled up to the curb, where they would wait for the morning bell before regurgitating students.

"I can see people." Emma squinted into the telescope. "I see Lily's ginger hair! Priscilla got glasses!

And I see Will. He's squashing his nose in a pig face against the window."

"He's in my class this year. I bet he'll be in trouble before lunch," Claire said disapprovingly from the next-lowest deck, where she was spinning the pirate ship wheel. "I wish *you* were in my class, Emma."

Emma looked up at Claire, and they both made sad faces. For the first time since first grade, Emma and Claire would have different teachers. Usually Claire's mom "secretly" met with the principal to pick Claire's teacher for "the right fit." That meant the nicest teacher. This year, Claire had gotten Mrs. Tingley, who was super nice and did Cupcake Fridays.

Emma had the new fourth-grade teacher, Mr. Webber.

Usually Claire's mother requested that Emma be placed in the same class, so the girls were surprised when they opened Emma's envelope one day after camp:

EMMETS/EMMA
Grade: 4th
Teacher: Mr. Webber

Emma wondered if Claire's mom had forgotten to request Emma. Or wait. Emma had a sudden thought. Claire's mom hadn't seemed so surprised when the girls told her Emma was in a different class. Maybe Claire's mom had made a different request this year. No, she wouldn't want them separated. Would she?

"I bet Mr. Webber is going to be funny and fun." Claire tried to make it better. "Maybe he'll have treats on Fridays, too."

Emma put her eye back up to the telescope and aimed it toward the next bus that was pulling up. She spotted Ethan L. in that faded blue baseball hat he wore every day at camp. Emma wondered if he'd be able to unglue it from his head for class. Hey, Rosemeen got her hair cut short! And there was . . .

Emma suddenly gasp-coughed. She looked twice to make sure she wasn't seeing things. Gleaming, long black hair, a smug smile on her face, shiny lip gloss . . .

"Isla," Emma sputtered. "There's Isla Cruz."

"Isla always takes the bus." Claire shrugged. "Her neighborhood's far. Remember that one party she had in second grade when her mother made her invite the whole class so we got to go, too?"

"Claire," Emma cut her off. "Isla's sitting in a *backseat.*"

"With the fifth graders?" Claire gaped, standing on her toes to look. "They never let fourth graders sit there."

Emma suddenly had a tight-twisted feeling in her stomach. She could picture the way this playground was going to be. The four high swings would be dominated by Isla and her three best friends. Or the pirateship jungle gym would become Isla HQ, where Isla would stand on the top platform like the queen lording over her kingdom.

Emma had a flashback to a moment from kindergarten. Emma swiveled the telescope to that exact spot where the old teeter-totter used to be. The spot where Isla had given Emma her first terrible nickname: Em&Em.

Okay, maybe that didn't *seem* bad, but then Isla had explained to everyone that Emma was the brown M&M that was poo colored. Poopy Em&Em, she'd said. This had led to Emma's second, even worse nickname: B. Em. (Say it out loud. Exactly. Ew.) All because Emma had jumped off the teeter-totter while she was at the bottom and Isla had been cherry-bombed to the ground.

It was an accident! Mostly.

Okay, a little on purpose. But there had been a reason for it. A secret reason that nobody except Emma and Isla knew.

Isla had never spoken to Emma again.

Emma shuddered. She had hoped this fresh new playground would wipe out bad memories. But maybe Claire was right—this year wasn't going to be *good* different. Maybe it was going to go all wrong.

Emma stepped down from the top of the ship. She sat down at the top of the red tunnel slide and slid, down, down, down. Maybe this year was going to be *bad* different, Emma thought, as her body slipped down around the first curve.

Emma kept her body stiff-straight, made the final turn, and felt herself speeding up. She could see the light at the end of the tunnel slide. Then suddenly, before she had time to react, a shadow blocked the light, and then a face peered up at her through the slide. Was that Annie Han from summer camp? Emma slid out of the tube and—

OOF! Flew right into Annie.

CHAPTER ♥ 3

Emma flew right into Annie's face, knocking them both over. OOF *and* OOF. Emma lay on her back on the mulch.

"You slid so fast!" Annie cried out, crawling out from under Emma. "Are you okay?"

"I'm fine"—*cough*—"fine." Emma spit-coughed out the dust from the ground. And her second mulch chip of the day. "Are you"—*cough*—"okay?"

"Is anybody hurt?" Claire suddenly popped out from the blue slide, holding up her phone. "My mom wants to know, too."

"I'm okay," Annie said, sitting up and picking a wood chip out of her sleek black ponytail. She brushed off her gray shirt and denim shorts and jumped to her feet, landing squarely in her royal-blue sneakers. "In fact, I'm better than okay. I'm the best I've ever been in my life . . . and it's all thanks to *you*, Emma Emmets!"

Huh . . . thanks to Emma?

"Henry and I are dating!" Annie squealed. "We're boyfriend and girlfriend!"

"You and Henry! Boyfriend and girlfriend!" Claire clapped her hands. "But wait, how is it thanks to Emma?"

Annie turned to Emma. "You tell her."

Emma would have been happy to tell her. But Emma had zero clue what Annie was talking about. The last time Emma had seen Annie was the last day of Happy Frogs Day Camp.

Emma was stumped.

"It's your story," Emma said generously. "You tell it, Annie."

Annie got a dreamy look in her eyes.

"So it was the last day of camp," Annie said. "We had Field Day, and Emma and I were on the red team."

"I'd wanted to be on the blue team," Emma said, sadly. Blue was her favorite color. Along with green (the favorite hue of her one true love, Jake LaDrake).

"Anyway," Annie said. "Emma turned to me and said, 'Annie, I have the perfect match for you: Henry.' And that's how it all began."

She sighed and smiled.

Emma thought back to the day in question. Their red team had been ten points behind, and Emma desperately wanted to catch up to the blue team.

The grand finale was the signature Happy Frogs event: leapfrog. All Happy Frogs teams were supposed to pick a couple to represent them. Emma had decided that Annie should represent their team, because she jumped higher than high in jump rope. And the obvious pick to leap over her? Henry "Long Legs" Hankins. The duo was a runaway success, winning the event and securing the red team as the champions.

"After we won, Emma said the magic words to us." Annie sighed dreamily. "*I told you so. You two are perfect together.* And Henry and I have been together ever since."

"Wow," Claire said as she turned to Emma. "I didn't know you were a matchmaker."

Emma was about to admit that she didn't know either. She only meant for them to be leapfrog partners (and she'd been right. They'd won!). Emma really and honestly was about to explain. But Annie spoke first.

"Oh yes. Emma looked around at all the cute boys and she knew, just knew, that Henry was the right one for me." Annie sighed.

Emma shrugged and tried to look modest. Instead of what she really felt: surprised and confused.

"It's like you have a superpower, Emma," Annie said. "A gift. A talent."

A superpower? A gift? A talent? Wow. Emma hadn't been particularly good at anything before, except spelling bees, which no one really cared about. Claire was good at basketball, Annie was good at hopping and jumping. Maybe this was finally Emma's chance for glory!

"So do you see two people and just *know* they're meant to be together? Like me and Henry?" Annie asked her.

"Yup," Emma said, hoping she sounded believable. "That's exactly how it works."

"You should be a matchmaker for our entire school," Annie announced. "People would be lining up."

"That's a great idea! Because I'm Em . . . Em-Matchmaker!" Emma agreed.

"EmMatchmaker?" Claire repeated.

Hey, that was pretty good. A big EMprovement over her other nicknames. Obviously better than B. Em.

"EmMatchmaker," Emma said, liking the sound of it. "Yup. Annie and Henry were only the beginning."

annie + henry ♡

"Wow. So did you matchmake Claire, too? Who's her boyfriend?"

"My boyfriend?" Claire squeaked and flung up her hands. "I'm barely in fourth grade!"

"Okay. Since Emma is practically a professional, she must know your perfect match, though," Annie said.

"Of course I could easily determine her match," Emma said. "But you don't want to match someone until it's the right time for them. And Claire has *years* before she's going to have a boyfriend. Right, Claire?"

"I haven't really thought about it," Claire said.

"Okay." Annie shrugged. "But you better not wait too long. When people see how perfect Henry and I are together, *everyone's* going to be lining up to see Emma."

Ooh! Emma liked the sound of that. She pictured another way the playground could be. The four swings could be dominated by Emma and Claire and, um, Emma's two new BFFs (to be decided later that day). Or no, wait. She'd take over the jungle gym. Yes, the jungle gym would become Emma's matchmaking HQ, where she would stand on the top platform like the queen lording over her kingdom, people lining up beneath her to . . .

"Emma? Earth to Emma." Annie snapped her fingers in front of Emma's face. "So who will it be?"

Emma sighed. "Me. It will be me."

"You're going to matchmake *yourself* next?" Annie asked. "Ooh! Juicy! With who?"

"What? No!" Emma snapped out of it. "Not me!"

"Then who?" Annie asked.

"Emma probably can't tell yet, Annie," Claire said. "She needs to see what everyone's like after the summer, anyway."

Phew. Claire had given Emma a stalling tactic. Annie would tell everyone about Emma's matchmaking. And, hopefully before she had to make any matches, Emma would figure out how exactly to do this.

"Exactly," Emma babbled on. "People change. Like, um, Rosemeen got her hair cut short! There will be lots of surprises. So it might take me a little while to make my matches, since the school year's new and all."

"I'm going to go to the flagpole and see if Henry's there," Annie squealed. "And, Emma?"

"Yeah?"

"I'm going to tell *everyone* what you did for Henry and me!" Annie grinned and took off.

"Wow, Emma," Claire said. "Annie's so happy."

She wasn't the only one. Emma was happy. Now Emma had no doubt that the fourth grade was going to be *good different*.

She didn't even know it, but she had a new gift, a talent, a SUPERPOWER! She felt like flying! And there was a place on the playground where she almost could. Emma ran back over to the swings!

"Twirl me!" Emma shouted. Claire grabbed her legs and ran around in circles, spinning Emma's swing round and round. Emma held on as the swing wound tighter and tighter.

Then Claire let go and . . .

The swing unwound, faster and faster. Emma tilted her head back and went round and round and round. She started feeling very dizzy and slightly sick to her stomach, but in a good way. She was so dizzy she almost didn't hear a teacher come out of the building and yell.

"Students! What are you doing on the playground?" the teacher yelled.

"We're taking it over!" Emma said under her breath. Then she leaned forward and took a flying jump off the swing. And landed right on her feet.

CHAPTER ♥ 4

"I didn't even know we were having boyfriends and girlfriends in fourth grade," Claire said as they left the playground and walked up the sidewalk toward the school entrance.

Neither did Emma. But if they were, then Emma was going to take the credit for it! EmMatchmaking could be her claim to fame and glory and happiness in fourth grade. It reminded her a little of a quiz she had taken in one of the magazines she borrowed (ahem, stole) from her babysitter.

QUIZ: *Are You Ready for Romance?*
- *You like the idea of "dating" someone*
- *You want to date because it feels right, not just because your friends are*
- *Your parents say it's okay*
- *You can be friendly, outgoing, and talk to boys*
- *You have other interests and hobbies besides getting a boyfriend*

"Why didn't you tell me?" Claire asked.

"I didn't . . . I mean . . . um . . ." Emma didn't exactly want to admit the truth now after the whole "superpower" thing. She looked around for something to distract Claire's attention. The sidewalk leading up to the school was lined with tall maple trees, their leaves just starting to turn from green to golden, red, and orange.

"Hey, tomatoes!" Emma pointed to the school vegetable garden, in a grassy nook near the side entrance. Small green tomatoes dangled from vines.

"The ones we planted last year," Claire pointed out excitedly.

"In third grade." Emma nodded nostalgically. She looked up at the red brick two-story school building's rows of windows. She could see colorful construction-paper stars taped to the windows of her old third-grade classroom. Emma guessed that on the other side, kids would be finding the star with their name on it just like Emma had last year.

"So anyway," Claire said as they passed the WELCOME BACK, STUDENTS sign. "Why didn't you tell me about Annie and Henry *dating*?"

Ring! Emma was saved by the bell. Chaos ensued.

"No running!" the monitors were yelling, practically getting knocked over in the rush of students.

All the walkers walked-not-ran toward the front of the school. The bus doors opened and bussers walked-not-ran to the front of the school. Everyone gathered at the front of the school for the traditional first-day-of-school welcome speech by the principal. It was the last thing they would have to suffer through before going inside.

But this was also a perfect chance for Emma to check out all her classmates!

"Hi!" "Hey!" "Hi!" "What's up, dude?!" It was a giant reunion.

Emma and Claire pushed their way toward the fourth-grade clump, when Emma felt a tug on her arm. Emma looked down and saw her little sister, Quinn. Quinn was tugging a large navy rolling backpack through the crowd. She also wore a pink sparkly backpack on her back.

"Emma!" Quinn said. "Where have you been?"

"I'm where the fourth graders are supposed to be," Emma said. "And now you have to go with the *kindergartners*. Over *there*."

"But I need to be with you," Quinn said, smiling her cutest smile.

"Aren't you supposed to be with Mom?" Emma asked. "And why do you have all that stuff?"

Quinn started pulling things out of her pink backpack.

"Mom said my first-day-of-school outfit wasn't a good idea." Quinn frowned, pulling out a silver tiara that she expertly slid into her dark brown shoulder-length hair. "She said I had to be an *undercover* fairy princess ballerina witch. So now I have to be undercover from *her*."

"You're hiding from Mom?" Emma asked. But as soon as Quinn slipped on a white tutu with sparkling beads and light blue fairy wings, it was clear her sister wasn't hiding from anyone. At all.

"Awwww, look at that little girl!" some fifth-grade girls said as they spotted Quinn.

Now Emma knew why her sister fought for the outfit. Quinn waved and smiled her sugary-sweetest smile. She did a twirl and everyone cooed.

Emma texted her mother with their location so her mom wouldn't worry. And so her mom would drag Quinn back to the little-kid area.

"Oh, she's so cute!" another girl said. A fourth grader, but *not* one of Emma's friends. The opposite of friend. The anti-friend, Isla Cruz.

Isla Cruz, with her super-shiny-never-frizzy long black hair. Isla Cruz, in her black scarf effortlessly flung around her neck, cream shirt, leopard-print flowy skirt, black cropped leggings, and brown slouchy boots. Her armful of bracelets, including three that said BFF. Three declarations of best-friendship, from three different people.

Isla leaned down and put her hands on her knees so she was face-to-face with Quinn.

"Aren't you adorbs?!" Isla said.

"Yes," Quinn said. "I'm in kindergarten. What grade are *you* in?"

"I'm in fourth grade." Isla smiled.

"My sister's in fourth!" Quinn said. "Are you my sister's friend?"

"Who's your sister?" Isla asked.

Emma cleared her throat. "Hi, Isla."

"Oh, hello," Isla said blankly.

"So! First day of fourth grade!" Emma babbled. Erg! Emma could never think of what to say around Isla and her friends. It was like her brain just got stuck, just froze.

"Yes. It is," Isla said. "Oh, there's Chloe!" And Isla walked away to her friends.

"She's pretty," Quinn said. "She should come over for a playdate with us. I'll ask her."

Arrgh!! No! But before Emma could protest, Quinn tutu-twirled toward the Isla Cruz Crew. Just when Emma thought it couldn't get any worse, her mother appeared. Emma needed to get her out of there fast and now. Parents were expected in the kindergarten area. They were *acceptable* in first grade. But not in the fourth-grade area!

"You need to go with Mom now," Emma said. "To the *kindergarten* area." Emma held on to Quinn's fairy wings so she couldn't make a break for it.

Mom stormed up.

"Thank you, Emma, honey," Mom said, then frowned. "Quinn, we talked about this."

"This is what a fairy princess ballerina witch would wear," Quinn insisted.

"She has a point," Emma said.

"Emma, that's not helpful," Mom said.

"What's the witch part of your outfit?" Emma asked.

One second later she learned the answer to that, as Mom leaned down to unzip the rolling suitcase.

"Quinn, put everything in here," Mom said.

"Don't!" Quinn yelped. "Don't open that any more!"

Too late. An oversize, floofy orange head peeked out the top.

"Winston?" Emma gasped. Quinn had brought their cat to school?!

Winston looked disgruntled as he tried to squoosh his enormously chubby body through the opening to escape.

"Ack, Winston!" Emma leaned down and nudged Winston back inside. He gave a weak meow in protest, and Emma could see his big golden eyes glaring through the tiny opening Emma had left him for air.

"Winston, baby, not yet," Quinny cooed.

"Not yet? Not at all. You can't take Winston to school!" Mom said.

"But Winston has to go with me! A witch can't go anywhere without her cat!" Quinn wailed. "He's my familiar!"

Emma said good-bye and watched her mom attempt to steer a protesting Quinn and a rolling cat-filled backpack through the crowd of elementary schoolers. Suddenly a furry orange paw thrust out of the backpack top and patted around. Winston's paw suddenly latched on to the bottom of a skirt. Uh-oh. Winston was tugging on Isla's flowy skirt. Isla kept talking and swatted in the direction of the tug.

When Isla felt the furry paw, she shrieked. She looked around wildly, trying to figure out what it was, but Winston's paw had disappeared back into the luggage as Emma's mom rolled him away.

Hee hee! The look on Isla's face when she felt the furry paw! Hilarious! Emma giggle-snorted so deeply, she started to choke. Emma left Claire alone for a second and ran to the water fountain for a drink. If Emma had known the water would burst out so high, she wouldn't have leaned in so close to the faucet. Water burst up into her nostrils.

"GLAK!" Emma nose-coughed. "Glug! Glurkle!!" Emma turned away from the fountain and let out a half gulp, half burp—"Glurp!"—and water-snot sprayed all over the ground.

"Ugh," someone said. "Gross."

Emma looked up to see a boy she didn't recognize. That was weird; Emma knew everyone. He must be new. He was really tan and had dark brown hair that spiked up a little bit in front. He was wearing a navy blue T-shirt, yellow-and-blue plaid shorts, and black flip-flops. Yep, he was definitely new, because he didn't know the no-flip-flops-because-of-tripping-and-injured-toes rule.

"Are you done puking?" the boy asked.

Emma opened her mouth to explain she wasn't

puking, but realized snot-coughing wasn't a much better answer. She shut her mouth.

"I bet you have first-day-of-school nerves," the boy continued. "You're worried about schoolwork, your teacher, your lack of friends."

What?

"I do *not* have first-day-of-school nerves," Emma sputtered.

"Taking deep breaths can help settle your nerves, maybe stop the puking," the boy said. "Just a little friendly advice."

"I don't need your advice," Emma said, frustrated.

"Go ahead and puke then." The boy shrugged. "Be the Girl Who Puked on the First Day. That nickname will stick with you for the rest of your life."

Erg!

"I'm just lucky you didn't puke on me," the boy continued. "It's bad enough being the New Kid. I don't want to be the New Kid the Girl with No Friends Puked On."

"I'm not going to puke and I *do* have friends," Emma protested.

"But they don't want to stand next to you because they're scared you might puke on them?" the boy asked her.

This boy was seriously getting on her nerves.

"Not only do I have friends, but soon I'm going to have so many friends that people will be lining up to hang out with me. It'll be like I'm line leader every single day with people following me around. Including you."

"Now I think *I'm* going to puke," he said and made gagging noises.

"Then I better move so I'm not the Girl the New Kid Puked On," Emma shot back. She noticed that the sticker on his backpack read *"Sabatino."* Mrs. Sabatino was a third-grade teacher. No wonder this boy was so immature. Emma was glad he was in third grade so she wouldn't have to deal with him ever again.

And also so she could say this: "Since you're new, I'll give you a little friendly advice, too," Emma said. "This is the *fourth-grade* area. You don't belong here."

The boy frowned, and to Emma's satisfaction he backed away.

"Emma!" Claire came running up to her. "Where were you?"

"Ugh," Emma said. "I just met a seriously annoying new kid. He thought I was going to puke on him."

"Oh no. Are you okay? Was it from too much twirling on the playground?" Claire asked.

"No, I didn't puke. I *wasn't* going to puke," Emma said. "He just thought I was. Although talking to him made me kind of nauseated. He was obnoxious."

"Annie's over by the wall, looking for you," Claire said. "Come on!"

Claire grabbed Emma's hand and led her through the crowd of people to where Annie was standing with her friends.

"Here's Emma, my personal cupid!" Annie said happily. Annie's friends swarmed around Emma.

Ha. If that annoying boy could see her now, surrounded by girls, he wouldn't call her Girl with No Friends. Hmph.

"Emma, Annie told us you found Henry for her," one of the girls said. They all turned to look at Henry, standing with his friends. He was easy to spot. His curly blond hair added inches to his already impressive height. He wore a gray polo shirt, khaki shorts, and blue-and-orange sneakers. And when he saw Annie, his face lit up in a big smile.

"Awwww!" all the girls cooed as Henry smiled and waved.

"Annie said you can find anyone's perfect match," one of the girls said to Emma. Annie's friends all looked expectantly at her.

"Yes," Emma said. "Yes, I can. I am EmMatchmaker. And I have a gift."

The girls crowded in closer to her. "Who's my perfect match?" a girl squealed.

Emma looked around at the crowd. No magical person popped out at her wearing a sign that said, "Me! I'm her perfect match!"

Emma needed to stall. She quickly came up with a plan. All the fourth graders would be together at lunch. Emma could check everyone out and decide. Then she could make the matches on the playground, at the top of the jungle gym where she could see everyone and everything.

"Now is not the right time," Emma announced. "After lunch, meet me on the playground. The top of the jungle gym—EmMatchmaker Headquarters."

"The first person to get on the playground should run and save the top of the jungle gym for Emma," Annie announced.

Emma liked the sound of that.

"See you all there," Emma said. "Emma Emmets, Playground Matchmaker will be ready."

Yes! Emma had her matchmaking headquarters, her time, and her customers. Now Emma just had to figure out one small thing: how to make a match.

CHAPTER ♥ 5

"Pssst! Emma."

Emma looked over at the desk next to her, where Rosemeen was trying to get her attention. Rosemeen had black curly hair newly cut short. She wore a light purple T-shirt and white skirt and had a stack of colorful beaded bracelets going up her arm.

"Annie wants you."

Emma looked up. Yup, Annie *was* waving at her from across the room and pointing at her bracelet. Emma squinted. It looked like one of the friendship bracelets they'd made in art at Happy Frogs camp.

"Henry gave her a bracelet he made," Rosemeen whispered. "Right before class started. Isn't that romantic?"

Henry was smiling at Annie, who was a few seats away. Annie smiled back. So adorbs! Emma also noticed lots of the other girls watching Annie and Henry enviously. Aha! Potential EmMatchmaker clients.

Emma was pleased with the way Mr. Webber had set up the classroom. Emma's first-grade class had sat at tables, where everyone worked in groups. Her second-grade class had sat in clumps of four, which could be great or not great, depending on who you were stuck with. In third grade, they had sat in rows, and it had been boring staring at the back of someone's head.

This year, the desks were in a shape that Emma had never seen before: a horseshoe shape. All the desks curved around in a half circle. Mr. Webber sat up front at his desk, facing them. He was wearing a green plaid shirt and a red tie with white question marks all over it.

Emma had a prime position at one of the ends of the *U*. That meant she could see all her classmates.

"Aren't Henry and Annie so, so cute?" Rosemeen whispered.

Yes. But Emma was watching them for reasons other than their cuteness. She was trying to analyze. What made Annie and Henry a perfect match? Emma needed to figure it out. And fast. It wasn't like there were going to be leapfrog contests in school today, where Emma would have to find partners for people who were small and bouncy, matching them with someone long legged.

What else drew Annie and Henry together?

Was it matching looks? No, because Annie was short and Henry was tall. Annie had shiny black hair, Henry had blond curly hair.

Was it that they both wore gray shirts? That would be nice, because Emma could just color-coordinate people into a perfect match. But no.

Was it personality? Maybe, but Annie was so bouncy and Henry was so laid-back. So was it opposite personalities that worked? Emma felt like her brain was going to explode. If she could just figure out the magic mystery formula for matchmaking . . . Emma daydreamed about the possibilities. People lining up just waiting to talk to her. People pointing at her and saying she brought happiness to the entire fourth grade. That's Emma Emmets! Emma Emmets—

"Emma Emmets? Are you with us?"

People were calling her name already? Emma snapped out of her daydream. Oh! Mr. Webber was taking attendance. He'd reached the end of the *U* shape.

"Hi!" Emma sputtered. "I mean, yes. I mean, here! I'm here!"

"Emma Emmets is definitely here," Mr. Webber said, and the class giggled.

"Fantastic! We have 100 percent attendance today," Mr. Webber said. "Now, let's turn to—"

He was interrupted by a knock on the classroom door.

"Excuse me for a moment," Mr. Webber said. "Please keep yourselves busy—*quietly.*"

The class watched as Mr. Webber left, but groaned in disappointment when they saw he was smart enough to keep the door open a squinch, so they couldn't go wild.

Rosemeen leaned over from the next seat and whisper-poked her. "Emma, look how cute Annie and Henry are."

They were cute all right. They were waving at each other from their seats and smiling. So very cute. Emma suddenly felt seized with pressure at the thought that she had to find two other people to be so very cute with each other. How would she pull it off? How?!

"Speaking of cute," Rosemeen whispered, "is that Jake LaDrake?"

"Yup," Emma whispered proudly. She tilted back in her seat so Rosemeen could admire her assorted school supplies: a Jake LaDrake pencil case, two Jake notebooks, and a smattering of Future Mrs. LaDrake stickers all over her binder. Emma's binder was flipped open to the first page, where Emma had written:

Jake + Emma 4ever

Emma LaDrake

Mr. and Mrs. Jake LaDrake and their
    lovely children, Sophia and Jake Jr.

Maybe Rosemeen didn't need to see that. Emma quickly flipped to a different section. Then she held it up to show Rosemeen how she'd sneaked her magazine with the full-size poster of Jake LaDrake into the "Misc." tabbed section in her binder. And that's when it happened. The magazine flipped open to the page on the back of the poster, as if by fate.

IS JAKE LADRAKE YOUR PERFECT MATCH? TAKE OUR QUIZ.

Emma smiled. She, of course, had taken the quiz and scored 100 percent. Okay, actually, Emma had scored 90 percent the first time because it turned out Jake's perfect night out was at the beach on a towel big enough for two—not at the movies with free refills on popcorn. But once Emma had changed her answer, then it was a 100 percent match. That's how Emma had known that Jake truly was the boy for her . . .

THAT WAS IT! Emma had it! Emma needed an EmMatchmaker version of this quiz! Then she'd have a guide to finding everyone's perfect match!!!

When Rosemeen had turned back to her own desk, Emma skimmed the quiz, pretending she was answering for Annie and Henry.

Huh. Emma realized something. Sure, she'd matched Annie and Henry because of their mutual leapfrogginess. But actually, it made a lot of sense. Annie was funny, smart, and liked sports. Henry liked to laugh, was smart, and liked sports, too. Maybe Emma had sensed it all along.

Emma could use this EmMatchmaking quiz to find everyone's perfect matches! She rewrote the questions so that she could use them herself.

Are You a Match? By EmMatchmaker

1. Do you have common interests?
2. Does your crush seem happy to see you?
3. Does your crush have the same sense of humor?
4. Is your crush nice to you?
5. Do you have fun together?

She was still writing her questions when the classroom door opened all the way. Mr. Webber walked in, followed by someone else. It was the new boy who thought Emma was going to puke. Hey, wait, wasn't he in third grade?

"Class," Mr. Webber said. "We have a surprise additional student. This is Daniel Dunne."

Erg. That annoying third grader was going to be in her class?

"I was supposed to be in third grade, but because of my exceptional test scores they're skipping me ahead," the boy explained to the class. "And with this state's cutoff dates, I'm only a month younger than some of you guys."

"Why don't you pull the extra desk over there to the end of the horseshoe," Mr. Webber said.

Fortunately, Mr. Webber pointed to the end of the *U* shape that was *not* next to Emma, but directly opposite her. As the noise from Daniel dragging his desk clanged and banged, Rosemeen leaned over toward Emma.

"Do you think the new boy's kind of cute?"

Was the new boy kind of cute? His hair was dark brown and spiked up a little at the top. He had the collar on his polo shirt popped, even though that was something none of the other boys did. Suddenly he looked up at Emma and caught her looking at him. And what was he doing? Making a face like he was . . . going to puke.

Seriously? Seriously. He was making fun of her? Emma shot him a nasty look. He grinned back.

Rarrr.

"No," Emma whispered back to Rosemeen. "He's not cute at all. Not even a little."

Emma would not look at that boy again. Ever.

CHAPTER ❤ 6

"Let's see if your brains are stale and slow after summer break," Mr. Webber said. "It's time for Webber's Winners! Each day I'll ask a trivia question relating to an upcoming lesson. Whoever answers correctly first will be Webber's Winner."

Emma sat up straight. Her brain was thinking now. Emma loved a good challenge, and she *really* loved winning one.

"What do you win?" someone asked.

"The winner gets to choose his or her class job for the day," Mr. Webber announced, and everyone cheered.

Perfect. Emma would choose to be line leader. She loved being the first in line and having the rest of the class follow her to lunch, recess, and specials. It would be the perfect plan to ensure she got to recess early enough to save the top of the jungle gym. She half-raised her hand in anticipation of answering.

Mr. Webber started. "And the question is: In poetry, how many lines are in a qu—"

"Four!" a voice called out. Everyone swiveled their heads to look at Daniel.

"That's correct," Mr. Webber said. "A quatrain is a poem that has four lines."

"But you didn't finish the question," Emma protested. "We didn't even get to raise our hands. That's not fair."

"I got the answer right," Daniel said. "I'm new. I didn't know you had to raise your hand. I shouldn't be penalized."

Maybe not, but he should be penalized for being super annoying, Emma thought.

"Next time, I'd appreciate if you raise your hand before answering. But today, I won't penalize you for not realizing this," Mr. Webber said. "Daniel is today's Webber's Winner."

Erg.

"I'd like to be line leader," Daniel said.

"Wow, you're quick *and* prepared. Did you have line leader at your old school?" Mr. Webber asked.

"Actually, I don't even know what it is," Daniel said. "Someone told me about it this morning, so I figured it would be cool."

Hey! Emma had talked about line leader to him. That someone was *her*. She'd ruined her own chance!

"A man who knows what he wants. Daniel will be our first line leader," Mr. Webber announced.

"Yessss," Daniel said, pumping his fist. Everyone laughed—even Mr. Webber. Everyone except Emma.

Emma knew what she wanted, too! And Daniel had just gotten all of it: the right answer, line leader—and everyone's attention. Emma wished she was in Mrs. Tingley's class with Claire instead of here with the world's most annoying boy.

"Let's take a minute to get to know you better," Mr. Webber said. "Tell us a little bit about yourself."

Emma perked up. This would be a great time to share her new matchmaker talent. When it was her turn, she could tell the class that EmMatchmaking would be open for business at recess. Annie might jump in and share how amazing Emma was.

"So, does anyone have any questions for Daniel?" Mr. Webber said.

Oh. It was "let's get to know about *Daniel*." Emma felt squelched.

"Do you play lacrosse?" someone asked.

"No," Daniel said. "I like wrestling and longboarding."

"Where did you move from?" someone asked him.

"California," Daniel said. Emma had never met anyone who had lived in California before. It was all the way on the other side of the country.

"Did you ever meet any stars?" Rosemeen asked.

"Sure." He shrugged. "All the time."

All the time? Now hands were shooting up all over the place. Emma had never met a celebrity before. Her dad knew one of the weather guys on their local news from his "good old college days," but he'd never even taken Emma to meet him.

Everyone was asking Daniel about celebrities. He seemed so smug about it. Like *he* was the celebrity. Emma would show zero interest in him, she decided. She leaned into her desk and started organizing her school supplies. Her pencils to the left, her green and yellow highlighters next to them, her Jake LaDrake folders in the middle . . .

Jake LaDrake. She looked up at Daniel. There was no way he had ever met Jake LaDrake, right? Right?

Emma tried to hold it in. But she burst.

"Did you ever meet Jake LaDrake?" Emma blurted out.

"Jake LaDrake?" Daniel said casually. "Yeah, I saw him at a restaurant once."

Emma cracked. There was no way Emma could fake zero interest anymore. He had seen LaDrake in real life.

"What was Jake eating?" Emma burst out. "Was it before or after his haircut? Was he wearing green, his favorite color? Did he—"

Mr. Webber cut her off. "One question at a time. And the goal is to find out more about our new student, not celebrities. Let's ask Daniel what *his* favorite color is."

"My favorite color is green, too." Daniel said. "*PUKE* green."

Wait a minute. Was he bringing up puke because of Emma? She looked over and he grinned. Yes, that puke reference was for her. Emma scowled. She realized she was biting her nails. Yes, Daniel Dunne was stressing her out and now she had bitten off one of the pink polka dots on her manicure.

Emma switched to biting her pen instead. She chewed harder and harder as Daniel started telling everyone about his favorite things and everyone listened to him.

Rosemeen leaned over. "Emma," she whispered. "Your pen—"

"Bad habit, I know," Emma whispered back.

"Thank you, Daniel," Mr. Webber was saying. "Now let's assign the other classroom jobs. Pencil sharpener cleaner will be . . ."

When Emma found out she was going to be door holder opener, she chewed on her pen even harder. Door holder opener was the worst job of all; it meant she would hold the door for everyone and be the *last* one in line.

When Mr. Webber directed the class to write a quatrain, Emma kept chewing on her pen. She wrote:

> If you're new in school
> You should follow our rules
> And not assume that
> You're so cool.

"Emma," Rosemeen whispered again. "Pssst."

Emma quickly crossed out what she'd written so Rosemeen wouldn't see it. Rosemeen was turning out to be slightly annoying also. Hey! Rosemeen and Daniel were both annoying, so maybe that meant they would be a perfect match!

Emma took out a piece of paper and wrote on the top:

* EMPM *
new secret code for
EmMatchmaker's perfect matches
Rosemeen + Daniel = PM?

"Pssst, Emma." Rosemeen poked her with her pencil. Emma ignored her, wishing that Rosemeen could magically morph into Claire.

"Do we have any volunteers to read their quatrains to the class?" Mr. Webber asked. Emma waited for Daniel to stand up and read his award-winning poem about meeting celebrities. Instead, Mr. Webber called on Henry.

> *"I met a girl at summer camp*
> *who leapfrogged into my heart.*
> *And now that we're together*
> *we don't want to be apart."*

Henry looked at Annie and she beamed back at him.

"Awwww," cooed half the class.

"Gross!" groaned the other half.

"Oh, I'm swooning!" Daniel pretended to faint and everyone laughed. Except Emma, of course.

"Uh . . . that was a surprisingly romantic quatrain," Mr. Webber said. "Who's next? Emma?"

Uh-oh. Emma looked down at her paper. All she'd written was her EMPM and the poem about the annoying—*ahem*—*anonymous* person who thought he was so cool. But Emma was saved from the embarrassment of saying she hadn't written a poem she could read aloud by a sudden burst of laughter. Emma looked around to see what was so funny. But it was looking suspiciously like everyone was laughing at her.

"Ha, she's green!" somebody said.

Rosemeen pulled a purple Bedazzled cell phone out of her bag and held the screen up to Emma's face. Emma had green ink all over her mouth and nose! Her Jake LaDrake pen had leaked when she was chewing on it!

Now everyone was seriously cracking up. Emma was sure her face wasn't only green now, but also red. ERG!

"Take the bathroom pass and go wash up," Mr. Webber said.

"I *tried* to tell you," Rosemeen whispered to her, giggling.

As Emma left the classroom, she was sure she could hear Daniel laughing the loudest. Well, ha. He and Rosemeen could laugh all they wanted. They deserved each other. No, actually they wouldn't deserve each other, Emma thought as she walked down the hallway to the girls' room. They were both so annoying, they would deserve nobody. Emma would cross them both off her EMPM list and banish them to loneliness for all of fourth grade.

Rosemeen + Daniel = Nothing

Emma stomped into the girls' bathroom and caught a glimpse of herself in the mirror. She had a wide green streak running from her mouth up to her nose and cheek. Hey, her teeth were green! Heh. She looked like a zombie frog. Even Emma had to crack up a little bit.

Emma washed off all the green ink except a tiny splotch on her cheek. She used her fingernail to make it into the shape of a heart. Well, Emma wanted to get noticed today, right? This wasn't exactly her plan, but she'd work it.

When people asked her why it was there, she would tell them it was her new logo!

Emma smiled into the mirror. Sure, people might be talking about her green pen-splosion but look what she could turn it into—promotion! She'd remind everyone about Henry's romantic poem and her matchmaking skills and nobody would be laughing then.

Emma sadly would have to toss away her Jake LaDrake green pen, but she felt that maybe he had a little to do with this new genius plan. It was like Jake was there, helping with her new matchmaking. If Jake were there, he'd say: "Emma, you have a gift, a talent, a superpower for making perfect matches. Like you and me."

Ahhhh.

If Jake were there, he'd take her hand and . . .

Actually, if Jake were really there it would be really embarrassing, because they'd be in a GIRLS' bathroom. Eeps! Emma had had enough EMbarrassing moments for today. She hurried out of the girls' room and back to class.

CHAPTER ♥ 7

While Emma had been in the girls' bathroom, her class had lined up behind Daniel and gone to lunch. Emma had to meet everyone in the cafeteria, running late. Emma carried her bag lunch over to one of the fourth-grade tables where Claire was already sitting with Annie, Rosemeen, and a few others.

"Skooch over," Emma commanded. She scrunched in between Claire and Annie. "We have much to do."

Everyone said hi as Emma unpacked her rolled-up ham slices, cheddar cheese cubes, apple slices, and—ooh!—a vanilla cake pop!

Rosemeen sat across from Emma with her hot-lunch tray (corn dog, potato wedges, baby carrots, and an oatmeal cookie).

"You still have a green splotch on your cheek," Rosemeen said.

"It's a heart," Emma explained. "I'm advertising EmMatchmaker. I need your guys' help. We need to get to the playground first so we can reserve the top of the jungle gym. That will be EmMatchmaking HQ. Got it?"

"Got it!" Rosemeen, Annie, and some of their friends all said. Claire, however, did not. Claire was chewing her pita with hummus and staring off into the distance.

"Claire?" Emma said. "Helllooo, Claire?"

"Oh! What?" Claire startled. "I wasn't looking at anyone. I mean, anything."

Claire was blushing hard. Blushing! Emma followed her gaze over to the next table . . . of boys.

"You were looking at somebody," Emma whisper-accused. "Are you crushing?"

"No," Claire protested, but she turned even pinker. Claire was blushing hard. Did that mean Claire was *crushing hard?*

"If you're not crushing, why are you blushing?" Emma leaned close to Claire. Claire turned a deep shade of reddish purple. Claire opened her mouth, but instead of talking, she quickly took a huge bite of her pita. Then she pointed at her mouth like, *sorry, mouth is full, can't speak.*

"Nice move," Emma accused.

"What are you guys whispering about?" Rosemeen leaned over eagerly.

Claire gave Emma a panicked look.

Emma got it. Sometimes you have to shush when you crush.

"Crushes," Emma said, and quickly added, "Other people's crushes of course. For EmMatchmaking. We're going over our genius plans to make everyone in fourth grade happy, including all of you. So may we have some privacy, please?"

The other girls turned away. Nobody wanted to interfere with the happiness of the fourth grade.

Emma thought back to a quiz she had taken in a magazine:

QUIZ: *Do You Have a SECRET CRUSH?*
FIND OUT!

Of course, Emma's crush on Jake LaDrake wasn't a secret. But Emma thought about Claire. . . .

1. *Do you feel nervous when you're around this person?*
2. *Do you sneak looks at this person?*
3. *Do you have trouble concentrating when this person is around?*
4. *Do you blush when this person is mentioned?*
5. *Do your friends notice you acting crushy around this person?*

Claire's answer would definitely be: YES! All of the above!

Whoa. Claire with a crush? Maybe it was happening because of all the fuss about Emma's matchmaking. Claire had never had a crush before. Well, except of course for the crush Claire had on three out of the four boys from the band the McBain Brothers. That was cool because it meant they spent time together, cutting out pictures from magazines and reading about their celebrity crushes online. But a real boy in their own grade? This was exciting!

And who? If Claire wasn't going to tell her, Emma would have to figure it out.

Claire had looked over at one of the fourth-grade tables, where four boys were eating. Emma thought about what she knew about each of them:

> *Jack*—Likes superheroes, wins burping contests
>
> *Ethan*—Super flirty, plays football
>
> *Kevin*—Emma's main competitor in spelling bees, otherwise quiet
>
> *Otto*—Weird, likes dragons, once got lost and ended up in the girls' bathroom

Emma concentrated. Using her EmMatchmaking skills, she decided that Claire had a crush on . . . who?

As soon as Claire finished chewing, Emma was ready.

"Ethan," Emma whispered.

"Huh?" Claire whispered back.

"He's your secret crush," Emma said. "Ethan."

"No!" Claire shook her head.

"He's not?" Emma said. Well, she *was* new at this.

"Then it's Jack," Emma whispered to Claire.

"No." Claire shook her head again.

No? She didn't even get it right on her second guess? Emma felt a little unnerved. She was Em-Matchmaker and she couldn't even pick out her own best friend's match? What if she couldn't pick out a match for—

Then suddenly, Emma saw something. She saw Kevin turn and toss a juice box into the air, into a high arc before it perfectly entered a garbage can halfway across the room. Then she noticed he had a T-shirt with a basketball on it. Basketball! Claire's favorite sport! AHA!

"It's Kevin," Emma whispered.

Claire blushed, giggled, and hid her mouth in her hands.

"It just kind of happened," Claire whispered. "He sits next to me in class. I was going to tell you, but it's so awkward."

"Don't worry, I understand. And I won't say anything," Emma whispered. She smiled at Claire, who looked relieved.

Emma wouldn't say anything, nope. However, it didn't mean she wasn't going to *do* anything about this. Emma wanted to see her best friend have the best fourth grade, and if it meant a match, then Emma was going to make that happen!

Claire + Kevin ♡

But not yet. She'd wait until later, after she talked more to Claire about this. In that moment, though, she needed a match that would go public *now*. She needed to make a splash.

Emma scanned the cafeteria. The first place her eyes landed was on Isla's table. They were squealing, laughing—and also sitting with boys. They would be a natural group to matchmake, and they kind of already had their boys right there.

Suddenly Isla caught Emma looking at her and rolled her eyes. Emma looked away. She'd work up to the Isla people later. She needed to start with someone a little easier, a guaranteed success. Someone who needed EmMatchmaker.

And that's when Emma saw her. Leah. Leah with her frizzled blond hair that few brushes could tame, her lavender sweatpants, her unicorn lunchbox. Leah was sitting in the back corner of the cafeteria, all by her lonesome. It was so sad! So lonely! Poor Leah, so very, very alone. Emma could make her a perfect match and bring happiness into poor Leah's life.

"Perfect!" Emma blurted out. Everyone looked at her.

"Did you think of a match?" Rosemeen asked. "For who? For me?"

"I did, but not for you," Emma said, then saw Rosemeen's disappointment and quickly added: "Yet. It's not for anyone at this table. I had to tune into my magic matchmaking powers and let them find the perfect match in this cafeteria for today's recess."

"Who? Who?" Annie and Claire asked.

"Leah," Emma said.

The reaction was not positive. It ranged from "Why her?" to "Who?"

"She's the girl sitting over at the end of that table by herself," Emma said.

"Oh sad, she's sitting all alone," Claire said.

"That means she has no friends and if she has no friends then how can she get a boyfriend?" Rosemeen challenged.

Emma paused. Hmm. She wondered if she had just given herself an even greater challenge than, say, Isla.

"EmMatchmaker is not only about finding someone her perfect match," Emma explained. "It's about making fourth grade . . . happy. And someone sitting by herself is sad and deserves a connection."

Everyone went *awww*. Emma was kind of impressed she had come up with that. And Emma realized that it was true. She wanted fourth grade to be the happiest year for everyone.

EMMATCHMAKER

Finding Your PERFECT Match + Happiness.

"Who's Leah's perfect match?" Annie asked.

That was a good question. And fortunately Emma didn't have to answer it, because the lunch-duty people raised their hands with two fingers up in the shush-up-and-sit-down sign. That meant it was almost time for recess!

"Yeek!" Emma said. "We have to snag the top of the jungle gym! If your class gets to line up first, be prepared to run for it."

"Please line up right here," the Lunch-Duty Lady announced, waving her hand. "The first class to line up will be . . ."

Please say Mr. Webber's class, please say Mr. Webber's class. . . .

"Mr. Webber's class," the Lunch Lady said.

CHAPTER 💘 8

"*Go*, Emma. I'll toss your trash," Claire squealed, sliding Emma's lunch trash onto her own tray.

Emma practically overturned her chair in her quest to get to the line first. Everyone from her class had to throw out their trash, but Emma headed straight to the waving Lunch Lady and made it there first!

Yesss! Emma practically yelled with joy. She was first in line for the entire fourth grade to go outside to recess! As her classmates lined up behind her, Emma made a game plan. She would race past the monkey bars and the zip line and then climb the quickest route up the jungle gym (up the steps, across the swinging bridge thingy, and up three more steps). Then she would claim EmMatchmaker HQ.

"Excuse me."

Daniel Dunne was trying to move in front of her.

"No cutting," Emma said, moving closer to Lunch Lady.

"I'm not cutting," Daniel said, attempting to squeeze in.

"No butting, no budging," Emma explained, angling herself to block him. "Whatever you call it in California."

"We call it cutting. But I'm not. I'm supposed to be first," Daniel said. "I'm line leader."

Emma sighed. This was seriously annoying. But Daniel was new; he couldn't know the rules yet. She supposed she'd have to be a little patient here.

"Line leader isn't for recess lineup," she explained politely. "It's for leaving class and walking down hallways but not recess. You'll have to go to the end of the line. Sorry."

Daniel did not go to the back of the line in defeat. Instead, he suddenly turned sideways and stuck one arm in front of Emma.

"Hey," Emma said indignantly. She moved forward, so much so that she was practically snuggling with Lunch Lady. And then Daniel tried to squeeze in between them and smashed Emma right into Lunch Lady's leg.

"Goodness gracious." Lunch Lady looked down. "What is the problem here?"

"She won't let me be first in line," Daniel said. "I'm line leader today."

"But line leader doesn't count for recess," Emma explained. "Tell him that's the rule."

"I'm new," Lunch Lady said. "I don't know that rule yet."

"It's a line," Daniel argued. "It's a line, and I'm line leader, so . . ."

"That sounds fair enough," Lunch Lady said. "You can be first and she can be second. Settled easily enough."

Emma tried to debate. "But—"

"It's just a line to recess," Lunch Lady said to her. "You may be second or else you may go to the back. Your choice. Does it really matter?"

Of course it did.

Ugh. Fine. Daniel being a teeny smidge ahead of her wouldn't affect her plan to reach the top of the jungle gym. Emma let Daniel stand ahead of her. She stood in front of Jack and told herself it didn't matter. But she couldn't hold back a frustrated sigh.

And then Daniel turned around.

"Your breath kind of smells like ham," he said.

And suddenly, it mattered again. Emma stood there, steaming. This boy was seriously annoying. Well, she'd show him not to mess with her. She could be just as annoying right back. She let out another sigh, this time a louder, longer one. Then Emma leaned in closer and let out another sigh, making sure to blow the air right at Daniel's head. She could see Daniel flinch. Heh.

"Hammmmm," she breathed at him. "Hammmm."

Finally, he turned around.

"Hey," Daniel said, annoyed. "What are you doing?"

Heh. It was her turn to annoy him for a change. Emma smiled in triumph as the final class lined up for recess.

"See you on the jungle gym!" one of Annie's friends called out to her. "Can't wait!"

"The jungle gym?" Daniel turned around. "What goes on there?"

Gahhh, why did that girl have to say that?!! Emma thought fast.

"Girl stuff," she said. "Um, the girls go there to talk about girl things like lip gloss. Boys hang out . . . uh . . . anywhere besides the jungle gym."

"I thought the playground was new," Daniel said. "How do you know where people hang out?"

"Uh," Emma stammered. "It's just something everyone knows, but you're new, so you wouldn't know. But anyway, you'll want to go somewhere like the basketball court."

"I'm not really into basketball," Daniel said.

"Then the zip line!" Emma burst out. "Just go to the zip line, okay? All the boys love that."

Why couldn't recess just start already? Emma was feeling the stress of just getting to her headquarters so her plans could begin! Fourth-grade matchmaking and happiness were almost within her reach!

And then suddenly Lunch Lady opened the door! Daniel walked through it first, but as soon as she crossed the doorway, Emma ran. Emma started running and didn't look back. She ran past the teeter-totter and ducked under the zip line and—

What? Daniel was running next to her!

"What. Are. You. Doing?" Emma said, out of breath.

"Going to the jungle gym," he said, running a few steps faster. "You want to get there so bad, it must be the best place."

Emma couldn't believe this.

"Go follow someone else." She looked around as she ran. "Why do you think I know everything?"

"You're like the know-it-all of our class," Daniel said. And then he ran faster! Daniel pulled ahead of her. Aw, man, Emma was out of breath! Daniel was going to beat her to the jungle gym! She needed that jungle gym to be able to scope out everything—and everyone—on the playground! How else would she find the perfect match for poor lonely Leah or all the other fourth graders who needed her?

Emma ran faster, but Daniel stayed ahead of her. Emma just couldn't run as fast as he could. She was exhausted! She couldn't keep up! Daniel was going to claim the top of the jungle gym and EmMatchmaker would be destroyed!

Then suddenly a blur of white and ponytail zipped by and raced up the steps of the jungle gym.

Annie! It was Annie! Yes!!! Annie had been the fastest kid in third grade—and now apparently fourth grade too! Daniel slowed down in defeat as they watched Annie bound across the bridge and up to the top of the jungle gym.

"Got it!" she yelled. "Got it, Emma! Come on up!"

"Ha!" Emma couldn't help but yell to Daniel.

"Whoa, that girl is fast." He shook his head in disbelief.

Emma didn't care anymore what Daniel said. She headed to the top of the jungle gym as other fourth graders came rushing across the playground to claim their swings, a spot at the zip line, or the basketball court. It didn't matter anymore!

"Annie, you're awesome!" Emma high-fived her as she reached the top.

"Thanks," Annie said. "Now, are you ready to use your superpower?"

"Yes! But first I need a little help with my super vision," Emma grinned. She grabbed the telescope and maneuvered it up to her eye. Annie, Claire, Rosemeen, and a few other girls swarmed the deck just below Emma and waited.

"Who is Leah's perfect match?" Annie called out.

"Hang on," Emma said, swiveling the telescope around.

"I knew she wouldn't be able to find someone," Rosemeen said.

"Rosemeen! If you're not going to be nice, then go somewhere else," Claire scolded.

"You can't rush superpowers," Annie added.

"Yeah," Emma said as she moved the telescope around. "And if you want me to ever use them on you, you better be nice to me."

"Sorry," Rosemeen apologized. "I take it back."

"Girls!" a playground monitor called up to them. "We all have to share. One more minute and then it's someone else's turn at the top."

"Hurry, Emma," Claire urged. Emma scanned around.

> *Swings*: Isla's group of girls with a few boys hanging around
>
> *Zip line*: huge line of random people
>
> *Basketball court*: girls and boys who were sporty—including Kevin. (Emma glanced at Claire.)
>
> *Monkey bars*: gymnastic-y girls
>
> *Bench*: Leah, reading
>
> *Teeter-totters*: spazzy boys getting in trouble for standing on them
>
> *Grassy area*: two boys pretending to sword fight

Wait! Two boys pretending to sword fight. One was Otto from her third-grade class. Otto! Otto was wearing a black T-shirt with a gold dragon and shorts that could use another couple inches. He had super-short blond hair and a look of intense concentration on his face.

Otto, who, as Emma overheard his mother say once, lived in his own fantasy world.

Just like Leah, who loved unicorns and fantasy books!

Do you have common interests?

YES! Otto was Leah's perfect match. "Perfect!" Emma said. "Absolutely 100 percent perfect!"

As she climbed down the steps, she couldn't stop grinning as the other girls excitedly followed right behind her, waiting in suspense.

CHAPTER 9

"There's one problem, though," Claire noted. "Does Otto want a girlfriend?"

"There's another problem," Rosemeen added. "Has he even talked to a girl in his life?"

Those were concerns, Emma silently agreed. She hadn't ever seen Otto talk to a girl before. But that was probably just because he was shy and a little . . . unique.

"Otto probably thinks that girls wouldn't be interested in a nerdy boy like him," Emma said. "I'll help him realize that is just not true. Girls have crushes on nerdy boys all the time. I myself had a crush on the Wimpy Kid from the books, before Jake LaDrake came along."

Everyone giggled.

"Emma's right!" Annie clapped her hands. "Emma, go use your superpower on Leah and Otto! Make them as happy as me and Henry!"

"Go, Emma!" Claire cheered. "Make a perfect match!"

Uh-oh. Emma had forgotten that part. She'd been so focused on *who* to fix up, she actually forgot she would have to go make it happen.

"Anyone want to play basketball?" Annie was saying. "Henry's playing."

Kevin was playing, too.

"I will!" Claire blurted out. "Um, unless Emma needs me."

It was better for Emma to try this without any witnesses, in case she crashed and burned. Claire was free to go stalk Kevin.

"No," Emma said. "Go ahead. I'll do this on my own."

Emma didn't know how. But she would. Yes, she would. Emma walked over to the grassy area where Otto and his friend—Emma thought his name was Marshall—were jumping around, pretending to poke each other with invisible swords or something.

"Hi," Emma said. Neither boy stopped what they were doing. Jab! Poke! Jab!

"You're dead, Master Knight," Otto said.

"I'm invincible, you can't kill me!" Marshall responded and did some elaborate hand move. "Not when I have my Sword of the Conquerors."

Emma walked over and stood right between them.

"HI!" Emma said.

"Is she talking to us?" Marshall asked.

"Yes, I'm talking to you," Emma said.

"She doesn't know she can't talk to us because we do not talk to mere mortals," Marshall said, allegedly to Otto.

"I just have to talk to Otto about something," Emma said.

"We can't hear mortals," Marshall said. Then he lunged at Otto, and their sword fight continued.

Fine. Emma pretended to pull out her own sword. Then she jumped into the game. Emma pretended to slice and dice up Marshall.

"What are you doing?" Marshall asked.

"Taking you out so I can talk to Otto," Emma said. "And you *can* hear me, because I'm Emma the Master Knight . . . EmMaster Knight."

Otto and Marshall looked at each other, not sure how to react.

"Are you challenging me to a duel?" Marshall said.

"I thought I just killed you," Emma started to say, but then Marshall jumped toward Emma. Oh, this was ridiculous, Emma thought. But as Marshall lunged, poked, and jabbed at her, Emma reacted back. She ducked, she spun, and then she pretended to knock Marshall's sword out of the way.

"I win!" Emma said.

"Wait, you didn't—" Marshall protested, but Otto interrupted.

"She is a worthy opponent," Otto said.

Emma studied Otto in his black T-shirt with its gold dragon blazing across the front. She had been planning just to ask Otto if he wanted a girlfriend and tell him about Leah. But now Emma had a different idea.

"Otto—I mean, Master Knight, I need to talk to you," Emma said. "There's a dragon loose in another part of this kingdom. See that girl over there?"

Emma pointed to where Leah was sitting, reading her book.

"She needs rescuing from a dragon?" Otto asked.

"No," Emma said carefully. Leah definitely didn't need rescuing. "She's fine, but if you don't do something soon we are all in danger. The only solution is to team up with a unicorn to defeat a dragon."

"Huh? That makes no sense," Marshall said.

"It will all become clear soon, Master Knight Marshall," Emma said mysteriously. "It will all be very clear."

CHAPTER ♥ 10

"How did you do it?" Rosemeen asked admiringly.

The school day had ended, and everyone was walking to the front of the school to catch their bus or walk home. Everyone including . . .

Leah + Otto

Yes, Leah and Otto were walking together toward their buses! Leah plus Otto sitting in a tree! Leah + Otto = LOTTO! Unicorns + dragons!

Okay, perhaps Emma was getting a little carried away. But she deserved to be giddy. Her first playground match had been a huge success.

"Nobody thought I could do it," Emma said. "I surprised you all."

"It's her superpower," Claire said. "Emma just makes it happen."

Well, it was a little more than that. Emma smiled, though, thinking about it. She'd taken Otto over to Leah. It had been awkward at first. Like a 9.5 on the awk-o-meter. At first, Emma had been the only person talking. But then she'd said something about

unicorns and dragons not being able to work together because they were natural enemies.

"Unicorns and dragons aren't enemies," Leah had
said. "Unicorns don't have enemies. Everyone loves
them, they're just impossible to hate."

"Not true, I've heard of zombies versus unicorns,"
Otto had said. "But dragons and unicorns can totally
team up."

Then the two of them started discussing unicorns,
dragons, knights, and who knew what else, because
Emma excused herself from the conversation.

AND NOW OTTO AND LEAH WERE TO-
GETHER!

Well, okay, if together meant walking to the bus
with Marshall following them. But they were talking! Now Leah had someone to talk to and Otto had
talked to a girl! And when Rosemeen had demanded
proof, Emma had asked Otto if he liked Leah. And
Otto had said yes.

"I have to give you credit, Emma. I really didn't
think you could do it," Rosemeen said. "Who's going
to be next?"

Emma saw the way Rosemeen looked hopeful. She
was probably hoping she would be the next lucky
subject. But Emma had had enough for one day.

"I just don't know," Emma said mysteriously.
"This was a challenge. I have to wait until tomorrow
when my powers have had a chance to recharge."

"There's Annie and Henry," Claire said.

Emma spotted Annie and Henry walking and laughing on their way toward the bus lines. Emma also noticed other people noticing. Annie and Henry were definitely the center of attention.

"EmMatchmaking, bringing happiness to the fourth grade," Emma said.

Claire nodded. "They do look happy." Emma noticed Claire scanning the area. Emma scanned, too.

"He's getting on the third bus from the left," Emma whispered to Claire. She watched as Claire spotted Kevin. Claire's eyes lit up.

HOW DOES YOUR CRUSH MAKE YOU FEEL?

☺ / ☹

Emma smiled. She knew that feeling. Tingly, buzzy, shivery, giggly. Every time one of Jake LaDrake's songs came on, every time she searched the Internet for a new picture of Jake, Emma felt that way. Of course, Jake was ten times cuter than Kevin or any other boy in their school, as well as unbelievably talented. But if Claire had a crush on regular old Kevin, Emma was willing to work with that.

Claire deserved happiness. Emma would work on this one. But she would have to be careful. Crushes could be very risky things—as Emma had found out the hard way in kindergarten. But she didn't want to think about that right now.

What she should be thinking about right now was her other responsibility. She had to find her sister and walk her home from her first day of kindergarten.

"I have to go get Quinn!" Emma said to Claire. "Text me later."

Quinn was easy to find. In fact, it was impossible to miss her. She was still wearing her tutu and twirling around so quickly, it made Emma dizzy just to look at her.

Emma turned on her phone and went over to the kindergarten area. Her phone beeped with a text message. It was from her mother, who said she and her dad were coming to pick them up. Emma groaned. She had thought she was going to be able to walk home without a grown-up. No offense to her parents, but she was in fourth grade now. She was supposed to be independent.

"And this is my big sister," Quinn told the girls around her. "She's in *fourth grade.*"

Emma smiled kindly. She remembered when she was in kindergarten, how big and intimidating the fourth graders seemed and how much she had wanted to be like them.

"You're short," a girl with dark curly hair said.

Apparently kindergarteners thought differently these days.

"*My* brother's in fourth grade, too," the girl said. "He's supposed to be in third grade, but he's really, really smart. His name is Daniel. We're new."

"Ah," Emma said. "He's in my class."

"There he is!" the girl shouted. "Daniel! Daniel! Over here!"

"Quinn, we have to go," Emma said. "NOW."

"Wait, you have to meet all my friends," Quinn said. "This is Mackenzie and Mitali and—"

Emma kept a smile plastered on her face, but inside she was frustrated. She wanted to be nice, but she did *not* want to see Daniel.

"And I forget her name and . . ." Quinn was going on and on.

Daniel was getting closer and—oh no—Emma's parents were closing in as well. Emma started backing away, but it was too late. They all converged at the same time.

"Mommy! Daddy! These are my new friends. Rachel and Avaline and Penelope and I forget her name and . . ."

Emma's parents said hello. And now, Emma thought, it was time to say good-bye!

"Okay, time to go, good-bye!" Emma said brightly.

"Rachel is new," Quinn continued. "This is her brother, Daniel, and she has a big sister and a lizard named Elvis who is going to be best friends with Winston."

A cat and a lizard, Emma thought. Now that's a pair you wouldn't want to match up.

"How do you like it here so far?" Mom asked Quinn and Daniel.

"Pretty good." Daniel nodded. "School seems cool. I got to be line leader and I answered a trivia question right, so I was Webber's Winner."

Emma grimaced as Daniel shared with her parents. It felt like Daniel was stealing her day.

"They're from Hollywood and they know movie stars and TV stars and singing stars!" Quinn added, awed.

"Have you ever met Jake LaDrake?" Dad asked. "Emma is obsessed with that boy. She plastered his face all over her bedroom. Even her bathroom."

"Dad!" Emma was mortified.

"He was at a restaurant right at the table next to us once," Daniel said.

Emma looked at Daniel's sister for backup confirmation.

Rachel nodded. "He even asked Daniel to move his chair so he had more room."

"Jake LaDrake *spoke* to you?" Emma looked at Daniel.

"Mm-hmm. He even sang." Daniel shrugged. "It was the birthday of someone at his table."

No. No way. This was enough to put Emma over the edge.

Line leader! Webber's Winner! Now he had also heard Jake LaDrake sing live?! Emma couldn't take much more of this.

"Jake LaDrake is on tour now," Daniel said.

"I know, I'm his biggest fan," Emma said.

"Are you going to his show to scream and faint when he sings?" Daniel asked.

Emma's face fell. "No, my parents won't take me."

"Honey, the nearest show is four hours away," Mom said.

"Jake LaDrake will be in the same state as me and I won't even see him," Emma said. "It's so wrong."

"Here. I'll sing for you instead," Daniel said. He started to play an imaginary guitar and—Emma could not believe this—started to sing. "I'm your perfect maaatch! I'm so perfect with my swoopy hair and my brooding good looks!"

He made an overly dramatic face that looked absolutely and totally nothing like Jake LaDrake.

Emma's parents and the girls cracked up. Emma crossed her arms over her chest and waited for him to finish humiliating himself.

"You're funny. You should come to our house for a playdate," Quinn offered. "Emma has a Jake-karaoke that she sings into while she looks in the mirror."

Quinn started dancing with an air microphone, also looking absolutely and totally nothing like Emma Jake-karaoke-ing.

"That's enough information, Quinny," Mom said. "We'll have a little chat later about what to share and what not to share."

"I better walk Rachel home," Daniel said. "Nice to meet you—bye!"

They were walkers, too? Emma had a tense moment thinking they might all walk the same way and Emma would discover that Daniel lived right next door. Thankfully, they lived the other way. Whew. Emma watched as Daniel and his little sister walked the other direction and out of Emma's life. At least until tomorrow. She could entirely forget he existed until school tomorrow.

"Well, he seems like a nice boy," Mom said. "Good sense of humor, too."

"Mrrfl," Emma mumbled.

"Let's walk over to the frozen yogurt place and you can tell us all about your days," Dad suggested. "Emma, how was yours?"

"It was . . ." Emma thought about it. "Good and bad."

"Ah, an emotional rollercoaster," Dad said. "When your emotions go up and down. The new boy said he was your line leader and was Webber's Winner. What about you?"

Ugh! Daniel again! What was Emma supposed to say? She was the door holder and had to go last? She was a Webber's Loser? She missed being in the same class as Claire? She sat next to annoying Rosemeen? She couldn't even get to be first going to recess?

"Let Quinn talk first," Emma said.

"Okay, so first we had to put any toys we had sneaked into our cubbies. Then she showed us where the tissues were and to throw them in the trash not in our desks because of germs," Quinn began her play-by-play. This left Emma time to fume all the way to the frozen yogurt place. Daniel was seriously annoying. Why couldn't they have left him in third grade, where he was supposed to be?

"Emma, tell us one good thing that happened today," Mom said, when Quinn finally took a breath.

Emma brightened up. She did have good things—no, *great things*—happen in her day: EmMatchmaker! Annie + Henry! Leah + Otto!

"On the playground, I got some boys and girls together—" Emma started to tell the story but was interrupted.

"Boys and girls together on the playground?" her Dad said. "In my day, boys and girls stayed separate. In fact, we had wars, boys versus girls."

"Girls rule, boys drool," Quinn scoffed.

"Now my little girl has posters of a pop star on her wall." Dad sighed. "They grow up so fast."

"Emma is in love with Jake LaDraaaake," Quinn sang, skipping along. "He's her cruuuush! Her booooyfriend!"

"In love?" Mom gasped. "Don't rush things. You two are too young to think about crushes or boyfriends. Anyway, Emma, you were about to tell us a story?"

Ooookay. Maybe her story of EmMatchmaker could be saved for another time. Or never.

CHAPTER 🏹 11

Claire: and he let me borrow a pencil!
Emma: ☺
Claire: a pencil he touched!!
Emma: ☺
Claire: i can't believe he sits right next
to me!!!!
Emma: ☺

"Wow, Jake, Claire really is crushing," Emma said out loud to the life-size stand-up cutout of Jake LaDrake that stood in the corner of her bedroom near her pink fluffy round chair and her white dresser with the lava lamp. As always, Cardboard Jake pointed and winked back at her as if agreeing.

Emma flopped back on her bed and sighed. Emma didn't really know Kevin. The only time he'd ever spoken to her was after he had gotten out on the word "significant" in the third-grade spelling bee (Emma had won with "syllable"). He had congratulated her and she had said, "Thanks."

Claire: kevin is soooo cute!!!

Claire: don't you love how his hair had those sun-kissed summer highlights???

Emma: yes

Emma: wait, no. you love that. I don't.

Emma: :/

Claire had been texting about Kevin for twenty-two straight minutes. Emma understood that when there's crushing, there could be gushing! But honestly, she was getting a teeny bit sick of hearing about Kevin!!!

It was like Claire didn't even miss being in the same class as Emma because she had Kevin instead.

Claire: sry. u must be sick of hearing about kevin. let's talk about ur superpower!

Emma: ☺ ☺ ☺

Maybe Claire's superpower was reading minds! She and Claire texted back and forth about how amazing EmMatchmaking was. They texted about Annie and Henry and Leah and Otto. Then Emma heard her mom.

"Bedtime!" Mom called. "Lights out, girls! I'll be up in a few minutes to say good night!"

Emma brought her phone with her as she climbed on her bed. Then she burrowed deep underneath her deep purple comforter and white shaggy blanket. Her head was down where her feet would usually go. The small light from her phone shone in the darkness, illuminating her bed-cave with only her screensaver, a picture of Claire and Emma crossing their eyes and sticking their tongues out of the corners of their mouths.

A new text popped up on the screen, covering part of their faces.

> **Claire**: if EmMatchmaking keeps going u
> r going to be popular
> **Emma**: :0
> **Claire**: people already are talking about it.
> u might be more popular than Isla! u can
> rule the school lol

"More popular than Isla? Rule the school?" Emma said out loud. Okay, Claire had put an *lol* after that, but still . . . could it happen?

Cardboard Jake smiled at her, seemingly giving her encouragement that maybe it could. After all, what did Isla have to offer compared with Emma's bringing happiness and perfect matches to the entire fourth grade?

Her cell beeped. What other wisdom and inspiration did Claire have for her now?!!!

> **Claire**: u know who lives on the same street
> as isla? Kevin

And . . . back to Kevin. Well, Emma would have to get used to this. If she was going to be in the perfect-match business, people would talk to her about their crushes. Emma hit "reply." Emma had avoided this question so far, but she knew she had to ask it sometime.

> **Emma**: so . . . do u want me to match-make? u + K?

Emma waited for a response. She just wasn't sure what response she wanted. *Of course* she wanted Claire happy. And if Kevin made her happy, then *of course* Emma should use her superpower on her BFF.

But . . . it was weird for Claire to have a crush on a boy. Emma was the one who always had a crush: on Jake LaDrake. Jake, the perfect guy. Not someone in their own fourth grade. Emma actually felt kind of weird about it. Was that . . . jealousy?

Emma's cell phone beeped. That would be Claire's answer. Would it be yes or no? Emma was about to read the reply when suddenly—

"Ouch!" Emma yelped as something dug into her back. Winston! Winston had sneaked into her room! She dropped her phone and heard it slide and clonk off the side of the bed onto the floor.

Winston continued kneading his claws on the comforter over her back, trying to get comfortable. Emma tried to slither out of the comforter, but

Winston plumped his chunky body on top of her. She was trapped.

"Winston," Emma whispered. "I know you're trying to get comfortable, but *ow!*"

Winston meowed a loud response. Very loud. Too loud. Emma heard footsteps approaching, and her light snapped on. Erg.

"Emma, come out from hiding," her mom said. "Oh, I see you're being held prisoner."

Winston kneaded again, this time into Emma's head. Ooooch. Emma buried herself deeper into the comforter.

"Emma, you're supposed to be going to sleep," Mom said. "And yes, I see your cell phone beeping on the floor, and yes, I'm taking it."

"First, may I just see that last text?" Emma asked, but her voice was muffled under the layers of comforter and cat.

"All I can hear from you is *mmmf, mmmmph,*" Mom said. "I'm going to assume that means 'Good night, Mother.'"

"But—" Emma protested. Too late. Her mom turned the light back off, and Emma was left in her room with only the night-light and no cell phone. Now she would never, ever know what Claire's answer was.

A crack of light widened at her door, and Mom's head poked inside her room.

"Claire texted: '*Not yet,*'" Mom said.

"Thanks, Mom," Emma called out.

Emma could feel Winston walk along her back to the end of her feet. Then Winston tunneled under the covers alongside her, his big eyes glowing in the dark like two little night-lights.

"You got me busted, Winston," Emma said. Winston knocked his head against hers, purring as he head-butted. Emma scratched behind his ears the way he liked it.

"I know, all you wanted was some love," Emma said. Then she paused. "I guess everyone just wants to be loved. That's why EmMatchmaking is going to be awesome."

Emma wondered who she should matchmake next. And after that. And after that! And then maybe everyone in the fourth grade. She imagined being followed around by a line of people begging for their perfect matches—and she wouldn't even have to be official line leader to get people to follow her around. (So *there*, Daniel.)

As she crawled out from under her bed-cave, holding it open for Winston, too, Emma thought about what Claire said: Rule the school!

Her mom was right. She'd better get some rest. Tomorrow would be a huge day for the playground matchmaker.

CHAPTER 💘 12

Emma stood at the top of the jungle gym, at EmMatchmaker HQ. She peered through the telescope at the almost empty playground. Emma could see the crossing guard, waiting for the onslaught of students to arrive. A couple of teachers straggling in late. Oh, and her mom, who came to supervise.

"Emma! Look!" Quinn called out. Claire was boosting Quinn up so she could hang on the hanging bar. Quinn's ruby-red slippers sparkled in the sunlight. (Mom had okayed the Dorothy touch. "One alter ego a day" was her compromise.)

"Cool!" Emma called back cheerfully. Emma felt much more confident heading to school today. In fact, if Emma had been in kindergarten, she might have worn a super cape herself.

EmMatchmaker was ready!

Emma peered through the telescope for inspiration. Right there was where Annie had first told her about Henry. Right there was where Leah and Otto had first talked. Who would be next? Emma decided she would let fate guide her.

She decided to close her eyes and the next person she saw would be the one to match up! Emma closed her eyes for a few minutes until she heard a noise coming from below. And the next candidate for matchmaking would be . . . Emma opened her eyes.

The custodian. Oops, no, she needed to clarify the rules. The next *kid* Emma saw. Emma closed her eyes again and opened them to see . . .

Isla Cruz.

"Hii!" Quinn's voice rang out across the playground. "Hii! Want to see my ruby-red slippers?"

Emma turned the telescope and groaned as her little sister jumped down from the high bar before Claire could catch her, staggered a bit, and then twirl-skipped up to Isla. Emma descended the jungle gym steps, crossed the bridge, and then slid down the fastest straight blue slide, which deposited her right in front of Claire.

"Sorry, I couldn't stop her," Claire apologized.

"Nobody can stop Quinn," Emma said grimly, watching Quinn showing her ruby reds to Isla.

"Well, at least now you have to go for it," Claire said.

"Go for what?" Emma asked her. "Oh no, you mean talk to Isla? About EmMatchmaking? Already?"

"If you find Isla's perfect match, you know everyone will follow," Claire said. "You need to take advantage of this. How often is Isla alone?"

"Like, never." Emma thought about it. Isla always was surrounded by girls—and boys. Claire was right.

This was her chance, and Emma needed to move. "Okay, let's do it.

"Emma!" Quinn called out. "Your friend is here!"

"Hi, Isla," Emma said.

"Hello," Isla said without interest.

"So, um, why are you here so early?" Emma asked. "Don't you usually take the bus?"

Emma shut her mouth. That sounded kind of creeperish, like Emma would say she noticed Isla sat in the back with the fifth graders or something weird like that.

"I'm the student representative for the Fall Festival," Isla said.

The Fall Festival? That was a pretty big deal. Every year, Happy Frogs Day Camp held a big festival on the school playground. Last year, Emma had won a ring toss and gotten a rubber snake as her prize. (She had recently renamed it Snake LaDrake.)

Emma nodded. "I went to the day camp. I was a Bullfrog. My little sister was in Tadpoles. Next year she graduates to Pollywogs."

Emma realized she was babbling and clamped her hand over her mouth.

"My parents donated some huge amount to Happy Frogs, so they asked me to be representative," Isla continued. "I'm sure they won't start without me, so I better go—"

"WAIT!" Emma practically shouted. "I mean, I have something to tell you. Quinn, show Isla how high you can swing."

"I can swing almost over the rainbow!" Quinn said, clicking her ruby-red heels together before running off.

"So, what is it you need to say? You're wasting my time here," Isla said.

Emma froze. She opened her mouth, but nothing came out.

"Maybe you can tell me later," Isla said, walking away.

Thankfully, Claire appeared at Emma's side.

"Emma, are you thinking of telling Isla about . . . *your secret?*" Claire said. Loudly. She raised her eyebrows at Emma. Ah! Emma caught on.

Isla stopped. "About what?"

"Emma has a talent," Claire said. "It's basically a superpower."

"I find people's perfect matches," Emma said.

Isla started walking back toward them. Ha! Emma had her.

"Do you know Annie?" Emma asked.

"The girl who is dating Henry?" Isla asked.

"Thanks to Emma," Claire said. "Emma matched up Annie and Henry, and see? Everyone knows about it. They've never been happier. And Leah and Otto?"

"Yeah, Unicorn Girl and Dragon Dork? That was unexpected," Isla said. "And kind of icky."

"Not icky, romantic," Claire said. "One moment Leah is sitting all alone and lonely, and then bam! Emma changed her life. And Otto's. Perfect match."

Wow, Claire was really selling it. She must have learned those skills from her mother the realtor.

"And you didn't even have to give Leah a makeover. Weird. Anyway, what's it got to do with me?" Isla asked. "Just because those girls couldn't find their own boyfriends doesn't mean I need anyone to do that for me. If I wanted to find a boyfriend, I could. Without your help. Obvi."

"I didn't mean you couldn't find your own boyfriend," Claire said hurriedly.

"We know you already have a fabulous fourth-grade life," Emma said. "But just think of how the *perfect* boyfriend could add to that. I don't understand exactly how my talent, my gift, my superpower works, but my superpower radar says I might be able to help you."

Emma and Claire waited while Isla appeared to think this over. Did Emma sound too silly? Superpower radar? Did that sound too far-fetched? Had Emma gone too far?

"I'm not UNinterested," Isla said thoughtfully. "But Annie? And Unicorn Girl? I just don't know if you're ready for, well, *me* yet. Although then again, I guess it was because of you I found out about the very first boy who was in love with me back in kindergarten. . . ."

And there it was. Isla had gone there. She had brought up the reason Emma had cherry-bombed her on the playground so long ago. The reason Isla had then called her a poopy-brown Em&Em.

The Day Emma's Kindergarten Experience Was Ruined

There was a boy in Emma's kindergarten class named Will. He was Emma's first crush. Emma had told a few people about it, including Isla Cruz. They had gone into action.

Isla had told Will, "Someone has a crush on you!" They let Will suffer in suspense for a few hours, and then Isla had written a note.

Do you like Emma? Pick one: Yes or No.

The note had come right back.

Do you like Emma? Pick one: Yes or No!

No, he had answered. With *an exclamation point!*

And then at recess, while they were on the teeter-totter, Isla had told her that Will had told her Emma was kind of weird. And then Will had admitted he liked Isla.

Not Emma. Isla. And that's when Emma had jumped off the teeter-totter, leaving Isla to slam to the ground and shriek so loud, everyone laughed at her.

Emma shuddered, remembering. She looked at Isla, being all smug and popular.

"You know what, just forget it," Emma said. "There are lots of other girls that boys will want to be matchmade with."

Isla realized she'd crossed the line.

"Wait! I didn't say no," Isla backpedaled. "I just meant you should perfect your talent a little bit. Prove yourself. Keep me posted."

"Isla! Isla!" Some girls came running up and pretty much whisked Isla away without another word.

"Well. That could have gone better," Emma said.

"No, it could have gone *worse*," Claire said. "She's interested! That's major! If Isla says yes, every girl in fourth grade will follow! But what was that thing about kindergarten?"

Claire had moved here in first grade, so she'd missed the entire episode. And even though they were best friends, Emma had never told her the humiliating kindergarten story.

Emma sighed. "I'll tell you another time. Right now, I need to focus on 'proving myself.'"

Isla had given her a challenge.

But Emma liked a good challenge.

CHAPTER ♥ 13

It was a good thing gym class was next. Emma needed to take out her frustration. She hoped they would play dodgeball so that she could throw the ball at Daniel's head. Or track, so that she could trip him. Okay, she wouldn't really do that. But it felt good to think about it.

Daniel had been Webber's Winner again.

Oh yes, he'd beaten Emma by one teeny tiny second. Then he stuck his tongue out at her.

ERG!

Emma sat on the second-highest bleacher in the orange gymnasium that smelled like feet. She sat with her classmates while Coach welcomed them to their first gym class. Well, not *all* her classmates.

Where was he?! Emma needed revenge. Then she realized that Daniel would be late because he had chosen to be office helper and was probably still delivering Mr. Webber's forms to the principal's office. Everyone always walked super slow and took long drinks of water when they got to be office helper.

Coach announced their lesson: swing dancing.

"Yay!" half the class cheered.

"Ew!" the other half groaned.

"In a minute, you'll choose your partners," Coach said, and then everything else he said was *buzz buzz buzz*.

Choosing partners! That meant boys and girls in pairs. This was an opportunity for Emma to prove to Isla that she knew what she was doing. Somehow Emma had to get in on this.

While Coach Scott talked about the history of swing dancing, Emma smiled as she saw Annie scoot closer to Henry. Obviously, they were going to be partners.

Then Emma leaned over to where Otto was sitting.

"Otto! Go sit by Leah," Emma said.

"Huh? Why?" Otto whispered.

"You need to make sure she's your partner," Emma explained.

"It's just gym class," Otto whispered.

"It's *dancing* in gym class," Emma said. "Dancing with a girl, so obviously your partner needs to be Leah."

Some people were so dense. Good thing Emma was there to explain it to him. As Otto slid over to where Leah was staring blankly out the window, Emma smiled triumphantly.

Annie + Henry. Leah + Otto.

"Aw, look," Rosemeen said. "It's like your clients are on a double date."

Emma smiled, observing how happy they looked. Other people were grimacing, groaning, and pretty much looking like they wanted to puke when Coach announced it was time to choose a partner.

"I'm leaving for three minutes," Coach Scott said. "When I come back, you better each have a partner."

Coach blew his whistle and then left the gym.

And the gym erupted into madness. Emma watched carefully. This was very helpful for Em-Matchmaking. If she was going to prove herself, she needed to make some more matches today.

Some boys and girls fled to the sides of the gym, as if the other gender had cooties. Other people looked around hopefully. She saw some people glance at certain people. Some people inched their way over. But nobody wanted to make the first move.

Emma realized this was her chance. She could step it up a notch, maybe even matchmake the whole gymnasium. Emma climbed up on the center of the bleachers and made an announcement.

"EVERYBODY!! I am connecting partners for swing dance! See me for your perfect partner match."

"Why should we listen to you?" a boy sneered.

"I am EmMatchmaker," she called out. "I have a gift for finding the right match. Even in painfully difficult cases like yours. With your attitude, it might seem like nobody would want to be your partner, but I will try. I may have to use bribes, but I'll do whatever it takes. Plus, we only have two minutes."

Everyone laughed.

And it broke the ice.

Some people waved their hands in the air for Emma's help, and Emma ran to them first.

EMPM time!

Violet was a no-brainer.

"Hey, I think you should be partners with Aiden," she said to Violet. "Go ask him."

"Me?" Violet squeaked. "I don't know if he wants to. It's too embarrassing."

"Violet, he needs you so *he* isn't embarrassed," Emma said. "Haven't you taken a bajillion years of dance at Miss Patty's Ballet, Jazz & Tap? Aiden trips over his own feet. Go save him."

Her pep talk worked! Violet went over to Aiden and—*tada!*—he said, "Okay." Another EmMatchmaking success story. Well, at least for this one gym class.

Violet + Aiden ✓

(And since Violet was friends with Isla, she could pass this along as more "proof.")

Nathan was next.

Easy-peasy. Nathan loved science, Kendall loved science.

And when Emma asked Nathan to be Kendall's partner, he said, "Whatever." Good enough! Emma practically dragged Nathan through the chaos.

Kendall + Nathan (ish) ✓

Suddenly people were calling out, waving, surrounding Emma. Emma was in demand! EmMatchmaker: Gym-Class Style! Woot!

Oh okay, it was just gym-class partners. So they weren't *real matches*, and some people were miserable that they'd have to dance with any boy or girl at all. But Emma noticed a few smiles, and boys talking to girls and girls talking to boys. Maybe for the very first time! You never know when a love match could be in the (sweaty, feet-smelling) air!

Rosemeen came over. "Emma, don't forget me. I've been waiting so patiently for my match."

Rosemeen, Rosemeen . . . who for Rosemeen? Emma saw Joe sitting on the bleachers by himself. Joe was a good listener. And clearly Rosemeen liked to talk.

"Go to Joe," Emma instructed, and Rosemeen followed with a smile.

Emma's talent was *on*! This was great, great, great! It was still going great when Coach came back into the gym.

"Does everyone have a partner?!" Coach's voice boomed, and he looked around surprised. "Well, huh. It seems you all followed instructions. I thought I was going to have to enforce some extra laps. Nice work, everyone! Except . . . YOU."

Coach pointed to Emma.

Emma realized her mistake. She had been so busy matching up everyone else, she didn't have a partner. And then when the gym door opened, she knew what was going to happen. It was all so obvious, so predictable. Why hadn't she thought to get herself a partner before . . .

Daniel walked in.

"You"—Coach pointed to Daniel—"you will partner with the leftover girl." Coach pointed to Emma.

Daniel and Emma looked at each other. Emma started to make a disgusted face, but then she saw Daniel's face. Was he . . . smiling? Well, not really a smile, but his mouth turned up at the corners as if he was not as disgusted at this turn of events as Emma would have expected.

Emma flushed. Okay, she would swing dance with Daniel, she would survive, she thought as she walked toward him. And if he got annoying, she could go with her previous plan and trip him or stomp on his feet.

"I guess we're partners." Emma shrugged casually.

"I guess so," Daniel said. And he smiled right into her eyes! And he reached out his hand to her before

Coach had even said they had to! And he smiled again.

AHHHHHHH!

And then Emma realized it. Smiling right into her eyes. Taking her hand (technically for the swing dance, but nobody else had yet done so). Did it mean DANIEL HAD A CRUSH ON HER?!

Emma took a few steps back with this realization. Whoa. Suddenly she felt dizzy. She had a weird tickle in her throat. Her body felt buzzy. What did this mean?

"I, uh, need some water," she said. "Be right back."

Emma bolted for the water fountain and gulped. She gulped so noisily she missed what was happening behind her. When Emma felt composed, she turned back to walk to Daniel. Her partner.

Except Rosemeen was there. Huh? Wasn't Rosemeen dancing with Joe?

"Um," Emma said. "Aren't you dancing with Joe?"

"He has a doctor's excuse to get out of gym," Rosemeen said happily. Then for some reason she winked at Emma. And then she looped her arm through Daniel's.

Emma was left standing alone in the gym. She looked over at Daniel, not that she cared or anything what he was thinking, but maybe he was going to give her a look like he was disappointed with this turn of events, but—

Daniel turned and small-smiled at Rosemeen, too. What?

"You're alone *again*? What, did you get ditched? Hahaha!" Coach's voice boomed out as he walked over to Emma. "Guess you'll have to be my partner, then. You can help me demonstrate."

CHAPTER ♥ 14

All eyes were on Emma and all giggles were about Emma as Coach grabbed her hands and moved them around and forced her to swing dance with him. Emma's face was burning with embarrassment.

"Small side step," Coach was shouting. "Shift your weight to the left! A one and a two and a—" Or something like that. Basically, Coach was flinging her arms around and half-pushing her into what Emma hoped looked like a dance. Finally, their demonstration was finished.

"Now that Emma and I have shown you how it's done," Coach said, "it's your turn. I'll walk around to watch your progress."

Emma took full advantage of this break and staggered, panting, to the top bleacher. There, she could watch everything that was going on. Emma finally caught her breath as she surveyed the scene.

✶ EMPM ✶
Annie + Henry
Leah + Otto

Violet + Aiden

Kendall + Nathan

And maybe even more than that, she thought as she looked at her classmates, observing how her matches went. If she could get one more couple out of this, it would be another successful day for EmMatchmaking.

"Rosemeen and Daniel, you've got it! Show the class your step-kick motion," Coach called out.

Rosemeen + Daniel

She hadn't meant that couple. Emma suddenly felt weird. Which was silly; just because Daniel obviously had a little harmless crush on her . . . Emma couldn't even finish that thought. It was all too weird. Okay! Well then!

Emma didn't want to watch but couldn't help it. Rosemeen was obviously using everything she learned at Miss Patty's, too—including keeping a big smile on while she was dancing. It looked like Daniel might have had that same lesson, too, because he was smiling a fake smile as well.

At least, Emma *thought* it was fake.

"Excellent, Daniel and Rosemeen," Coach called out. "Now let's all try. Where's my partner?"

Emma + Coach

Arrrrrgggggggg!

CHAPTER ♥ 15

Claire had gym after lunch. Emma silently chomped on her tuna fish sandwich, as Rosemeen filled Claire in on the wonders of EmMatchmaking in gym class.

"So then, Coach says, 'Pick your partner,'" Rosemeen said. "And then Emma used her superpowers to match a bunch of people up."

"Wow," Claire said. "Who was your match?"

"Rosemeen's wasn't a *real* match," Emma said, even though her mouth was full.

"At first," Rosemeen agreed. "Emma put me with Joe, but it was just a stalling tactic. Somehow, Emma knew that Joe couldn't take gym and my real match was coming in late."

Emma choked on her sandwich.

"My perfect match is Daniel!" Rosemeen said.

"Daniel?" Claire looked at Emma. "Really? That's who Emma picked for your perfect match?"

"NO!" Emma said. "Just for gym class! A gym-class match!"

It wasn't like Emma had picked him for Rosemeen. He was supposed to be Emma's partner. Not that she particularly wanted him to be or anything.

Emma wiped her mouth on her Jake LaDrake napkin. She took a moment to appreciate how Jake even looked cute with a mustard smear over his face.

"You *don't* think Daniel's my perfect match?" Rosemeen looked confused. "We had such natural chemistry! Didn't you hear what Coach said about how great we danced together?"

"Daniel dances?" Claire asked.

Rosemeen nodded. "His mother made him take classes. Daniel said a lot of kids take dance in LA in case they want to audition and be TV stars."

Emma steered the conversation back in the right direction. "So, sorry, but I don't think he's your perfect match, Rosemeen. I just knew you'd want a good dance partner. Your *real* perfect match isn't in our class."

"Who is it?" Rosemeen asked eagerly.

"Um, I'm not one hundred percent sure yet," Emma said. "But my powers are telling me I'm close. In fact, I'm looking right now. . . ."

The girls all looked around the cafeteria.

A loud burst of laughter came from the lunch table in the center. Everyone turned around to look. Isla and her friends were laughing about something.

"I wonder who Isla's dance partner will be," Rosemeen said. "I bet every guy is going to ask her."

"Emma talked to Isla about finding her perfect match this morning," Claire said.

"Seriously?" Rosemeen said, turning to Emma. "What did she say?"

"She said she's definitely 'not uninterested,'" Emma said. Emma didn't think it was necessary to add anything about having to prove herself.

"Whoa," Rosemeen said. "Next time she talks to you, make sure you get me. I haven't talked to Isla Cruz since we both had to get our eyes checked in first grade at the same time. I told her the letters on the third row so she wouldn't have to get glasses."

"You know what, you'd be a good friend for Isla," Emma blurted.

"That was random," Claire said.

"Me? A friend for Isla?" Rosemeen asked. "What do you mean?"

"Um," Emma said. "I don't know. It just popped into my head."

"What are you, a friend matchmaker?" Rosemeen said. "Besides, Isla has all her cool-people friends. Why would she want me?"

"I told you, it just popped into my head," Emma repeated and shrugged.

"Anyway, Claire, you better ask Emma to help find your swing dance partner," Rosemeen warned. "You want to be ready when Coach says to pick your partner. Maybe you should go ask someone at recess."

Claire looked at Emma. Emma knew Claire was thinking about Kevin.

"Are you going to ask him?" Emma whispered.

"I can't," Claire whispered. "I'm scared. What if he says no?"

Claire always had Emma's back. Emma needed to have Claire's back, too. Claire wouldn't do this by herself. It would be up to Emma.

The Lunch Lady pointed to their table, and as they cleaned up their trays, Emma thought quickly. She let Claire go first and then blocked Rosemeen and Annie.

"Meet you at the jungle gym?" Rosemeen said.

"Actually, I need to scope the playground," Emma said. "ALONE. To, um, get the best vibe. Can you guys *and Claire* go to the swings or zip line or something instead?"

"Sure," Annie said. "Or we can go play basketball. Henry will play with us."

"NO!" Emma said. "I mean, anywhere but the basketball court for a while, okay?"

Annie shrugged. "Anything for EmMatchmaker. Maybe Henry will want to swing with me."

"Aw, that's so sweet," Rosemeen said.

With that, Emma headed out the door alone. She made her way across the playground. Past the jungle gym, the teeter totters, the grass patch where Leah, Otto, and Marshall were deep in fantasyland. Emma got to the basketball court just in time—as Kevin was walking near.

"Hey, Kevin?" Emma called out. "Kevin?"

"Yeah?" Kevin stopped.

Emma had a moment of panic. What if she screwed things up for Claire? What if she made things worse?

Then again, what if Kevin asked someone else to swing dance and then Claire never had her shot? Claire could be brokenhearted as Kevin swing danced away with some other girl. Emma had a superpower, a gift, a talent, and who better to use it for than your very best friend!

"Kevin, in gym class today, you guys are going to do swing dancing," Emma said.

"Aw, seriously?" Kevin said. "Ugh. That's gross."

Emma didn't know Kevin well enough to know what appealed to him. Was he competitive?

"And you have to have a partner," Emma continued. "Since it's so gross already, don't you want a partner who's a really good dancer so you guys can be the best?"

Kevin shrugged. "At swing dancing? Not really."

Okay, new approach.

"Hey, it's a special day for someone in your class. So can you do something nice for her?" Emma asked.

"For a birthday? Sure," Kevin said. "Birthdays are really important."

"Not exactly a birthday," Emma hedged. She didn't like to lie, so hopefully he wouldn't push it. It *would* be a special day if Kevin would ask Claire to dance. "Just a . . . special day. If you asked her to be your partner, that would be great."

"Why? Why me?" Kevin asked.

Emma gave him a knowing look. Kevin gave her a

confused look. All righty, he wasn't getting the hint. Emma obviously didn't want to come out and say Claire had a crush on him.

"Remember when we did the spelling bee and even though I squashed your dreams of going on to regionals, you congratulated me?" Emma asked. "That showed you are a nice person. I want my friend to have someone nice to dance with on her special day."

Emma looked at him hopefully. Did that work?

"All right," Kevin said with a shrug.

"You will?" Emma squealed, then controlled herself. "Of course you will. Thanks! Awesome! Great! You can go play basketball now."

"Uh, you forgot to tell me who I'm supposed to ask," Kevin said.

Oops!

"Claire," Emma said. And Kevin responded, "Okay."

Okay! He said okay! Emma cheered in her head as Kevin went off to play basketball. Oh, this was fantastic. Emma practically skipped back over to the line for the zip line, where Claire was waiting with Rosemeen and Annie.

"Where were you?" Claire asked. "Looking around for people to match up?"

"Yes," Emma said. "Yes, I was."

Emma couldn't wait for Claire to find out what was going to happen! Emma had a good feeling about this. She pictured Kevin asking Claire to dance.

They'd dance! Then they would become boyfriend/
girlfriend! Then they'd get married!

Emma was so pleased, she leaned over and spon-
taneously hugged a surprised Claire.

"Hey! No cutting!" the boy behind them said.

"I'm just cheering my friend on," Emma said.
And as Claire zipped down the zip line, Emma
cheered—loudly.

CHAPTER ♥ 16

Claire: !!!!!!
Emma: ☺
Claire: !!!!!!
Emma: ☺

"No texting during family meals," Quinn said, cheerfully busting Emma as she held her cell under the dinner table.

"Sorry." Emma shot Quinn a look. "It's important."

It was important! They were celebrating. Yes, Kevin had asked Claire to be his swing dance partner! When Claire had excitedly told Emma, she had then said, "Do you have anything to do with this?"

"Yes," Emma said with a wince, hoping Claire would be okay with it, since she'd said not to match her yet and all. "I thought the moment was right."

Thankfully, Claire had thrown her arms around Emma.

"You really do have a superpower," Claire told Emma. "Thank you so much for using it on me!"

Phew.

Claire: ☺

"Are you texting about schoolwork?" Mom asked. "Are you feeling pressured with homework already? Do you want me to help you? Do you need a tutor?"

"I'm fine, Mom," Emma said.

"Are you texting a boy?" Quinn asked and then slurped her pasta.

"Quinn!" Dad said. "No slurping. You're getting noodle juice all over your princess gown. And Emma? You're texting boys?"

"I'm *not*," Emma said. "I'm texting Claire."

"My friend Phoebe said her big sister said that Emma is getting really popular," Quinn said. "She is asking all the boys to be boyfriends."

"WHAT?!" The table erupted as her parents looked at her.

"I'm not!" Emma protested. "I didn't ask anyone to be my boyfriend!"

She had asked people to be *other people's* boyfriends, but Emma wasn't sure how to explain that one to her parents yet.

"We had swing dancing in gym and we had to have partners," Emma explained. "I'm just trying to get everyone to know each other better and be happy."

"Well, that sounds like a worthy goal," Dad said. "Quinn, perhaps you can ask your friend to rephrase what she said about your sister a little better, so it's more accurate."

"Who was your partner, Emma?" Quinn asked, shoving a big heap of pasta on her fork.

"Coach," Emma mumbled. Then she brightened. "See? If I had a boyfriend, I wouldn't have to have been partnered with the gym teacher."

"You can go out with my friend's brother," Quinn offered. "Rachel said her brother Daniel thinks you're smart."

Emma dropped her fork.

"Daniel talked about me?" Emma said.

"That's what Rachel said he told their parents," Quinn shrugged. "She said he said so at dinner last night!"

Mom turned to Emma. "Of course you're smart. You're smart and beautiful, inside and out."

Mom went off on one of her self-esteem talks, while Emma thought about what Quinn had said. Daniel talked about her to his sister and parents. Interesting. Emma reflected on the look on Daniel's face when he was originally supposed to be Emma's dance partner, before Rosemeen had stolen him.

Daniel had smiled, she just knew it. Daniel was talking about her. Daniel had been thinking of her. Daniel had a crush.

CHAPTER 💘 17

The following day, Emma's class was last to go out to the playground at recess. But when Emma arrived at the jungle gym, planning to wait for a turn at the top, she had a surprise. "Emma! Come up! We're saving it for you!"

"Do I even know those girls?" Emma asked Claire, squinting. Claire shook her head as they climbed to the top.

"We saved EmMatchmaker HQ for you," a girl Emma vaguely recognized said. She looked at her friend. "We're first in line! We're ready for you."

Line? Emma looked at the line of people winding their way up the jungle gym. Were they all here for EmMatchmaking?!?!!

"Are you all here for EmMatchmaking?!" Emma called down.

"Yes!" a handful said. The others shook their heads no. Oh. They were just waiting to be at the top of the jungle gym. Okay, so she didn't exactly have a line. But she still had people waiting for her! Emma felt so EMportant!

Emma grinned. The playground matchmaker was open for business!

"Now, just because you come to me doesn't mean my superpower is ready for you yet," Emma said. "Matches take time; it doesn't always work immediately. But it does mean I'll think about your match and then go to work making it happen."

The first one was a piece of cake. Really. The first girl liked baking and decorating cakes. Match-caking! Match-baking! Emma planned to matchmake her with a boy who always traded his lunch for other people's desserts.

Next, a boy came up to the top.

"Hi," he said. "I like someone."

"Who?" Emma asked, peering through the telescope. She didn't have to peer far.

"That girl," the boy said. He pointed at a girl who was looking up at him, smiling and waving and pointing at herself.

"I don't think that's going to be a problem," Emma said.

Another girl liked art. Emma looked around through the telescope, adjusting focus until she spotted a boy who was drawing in chalk on the cement. There were so many people that Emma had Claire keep careful track of them on the EMPM list.

Business was booming! Emma was thrilled.

"Wowzers. Word is getting around about your talent," Claire said. Then she raised her voice: "NEXT!"

The next person to climb up into EmMatch-maker HQ took both of them by surprise. First, they glimpsed a fashionably messy bun of black hair rising up. Then they saw a serious-looking face.

Isla Cruz. Wearing a yellow summer dress with a coral scarf flung around her neck perfectly so.

"Thank you for coming to EmMatchmaker. How may I help you?" Emma flushed. It sounded like she was asking to take Isla's order for a burger and fries.

"I've seen your work," Isla said, tilting her head and studying Emma. "I thought you might be a fluke, but even my friends were talking about your skills in gym class. And I don't mean your dancing with Coach."

EMbarrassing.

"Remember when I told you I was the student representative for the Fall Festival?" Isla asked. "One of my responsibilities is finding fresh ideas for new booths."

"Ooh, how about a petting zoo?" Claire said. "Can we have a petting zoo? Or how about pie throwing, where, like, I'd throw a pie in your face to win—"

"*I* meant *I'm* thinking of ideas," Isla interrupted.

"Sorry," Claire squeaked.

"I'm considering suggesting a matchmaking booth," Isla went on, then paused and looked at Emma.

"You're going to be a matchmaker, too?" Claire

asked her, shooting Emma a worried look. "Are you going to compete against Emma?"

"No, I was already asked to be a model for the department store's fashion show," Isla said. "So I'm booked for the festival. Obvi, Emma can run the matchmaker booth."

Seriously?

"I'd have my own booth?" Emma said. Whoa. Everyone went to the Fall Festival. That would be huge for EmMatchmaking. Emma could picture the booth, her name splashed across the top:

EMMA EMMETS,
PLAYGROUND MATCHMAKER

The Happy Frogs Fall Festival was a big deal. There were shows and rides, food and games and prizes. *Everyone* went to it!

"Wait. What's in it for you, then?" Emma asked. "If you're not going to be part of the matchmaking booth, I mean."

"People are starting to talk about you," Isla said.

"So if you set up my booth, it looks like *you* discovered me," Emma said, catching on. "You get some credit."

"Well, obvi, you'll tell people the booth was my idea," Isla said. "It's a win for both of us. "

"So, you're impressed now, right?" Emma said. "Last time you said you 'weren't UNimpressed.' Are you impressed enough for me to make *your* perfect match?"

Isla looked thoughtful.

"Not quite yet," Isla said. "Let's see how things go at the meeting Friday. If you have any other success stories by then, tell me so I can use it to convince the committee."

Emma was planning to have that meeting go well. Very, very well. By Friday, Emma needed to make a big splash. She would do whatever it took to prove herself. Emma wanted that matchmaking booth.

What could Emma do that would make everyone stand up and take notice?

"You should be impressed," Claire said. "I mean, look over there at Henry and Annie on the teeter-totter. So cute! They're practically married."

Married. *Married!*

And Emma suddenly knew what she was going to do.

CHAPTER ♥ 18

"Will you tell me your idea now?" Claire called out from Emma's room, where she was waiting. Emma had invited Claire over after school with a plan to convince her to go along with her mysterious Big Idea.

"Just a minute," Emma said cheerfully, walking up the stairs while carefully holding a tray. She went into her room and set the tray down on her bedside table. Claire was sitting on Emma's bed. Winston was flopped over next to her, with his neck positioned perfectly for Claire to scratch him under his collar.

"Wow," Claire said, eyeing the tray. On it were:

* Brownies
* Sliced strawberries
* A bowl of whipped cream
* Ruffly sour cream–and–
  onion chips

"I just thought that after a hard day of school, you needed a treat," Emma said. Winston must have thought the same thing, because he attempted to stick his furry paw into the whipped cream.

Claire pulled Winston away and put him on her lap. Winston rolled onto his back and splayed his legs out, one eye open and waiting. Claire began scratching him on his belly, and his eye closed. Winston loudly motor-purred with happiness.

"Does this have something to do with your Big Idea? Are you going to try to talk me into something? You can't just bribe me with food, you know." Claire frowned. Then she brightened and pulled her phone out of her pocket.

"Is that Kevin?" Emma asked.

"Yes!" Claire smiled. "He sent me a funny picture of a cow."

She stopped scratching Winston as she texted. Kevin texted. Claire texted. Winston stopped purring and batted at Claire's phone, trying to get her to focus on him again.

Emma knew how Winston felt.

"Claire?" Emma said. "Don't you want to know the Big Idea?"

"Yes!" Claire said, texting.

"It's a wedding!" Emma said. "A playground wedding."

"Cool," Claire said absently.

"A playground wedding for you and Kevin."

"Cool," Claire said. Then she looked up. "Wait, what?"

"A wedding," Emma said. "YOUR wedding to Kevin."

If Emma had any advance warning that Quinn was going to burst into her bedroom without knocking, Emma wouldn't have taken such a huge sip of the juice pouch. Berry-kiwi juice sprayed out of her nose and all over her bed.

"Glak!" Emma gasp-coughed. Then she gasped. Berry-kiwi juice-snot did not match her pale pink comforter.

"QUINN!" Emma shouted.

"What's this about a wedding?" Quinn stood with her hands on her hips—and a police hat on her head and a pirate's patch over one eye.

Emma groaned. "Quinn, you're supposed to knock." Winston spotted Quinn and tried to bolt out the open door, but Quinn was too quick for him. She reached down and scooped him up in her arms.

"Hi, Winnie shmoopie boop," Quinn cooed, holding Winston with full force in her arms. Winston gave up and went limp, dangling in her arms like an enormous floppy orange sock.

"Hi, Q," Claire said.

"You're getting married to Kevin?" Quinn asked. "Isn't that kind of fast? I thought you just started dating."

"Not a *real* wedding. A playground wedding," Emma said. Then she looked at Quinn. "But wait, how do you know Claire is dating anyone?"

"I hear things," Quinn said with a shrug. "When's the wedding? Ooh, Claire, you'll be such a pretty bride!"

Emma realized that she had an unexpected ally. She pointed to the tray.

"Have a snack," Emma said. "Stay a while."

"Can I be a flower girl? Can I wear a light purple dress and high heels?" Quinn bounced over to the bed and sat down, plopping Winston on her lap. "Can Winston be the ring cat?"

"Wait," Claire protested. "I didn't say I'd do a wedding!"

"Claire," Emma said. "You love weddings. You made me play weddings with our monster dolls, our Barbies, and even our baby dolls."

"That was a little weird," Claire admitted. "Babies in wedding dresses."

"You watch people shopping for wedding dresses on TV," Emma continued.

"Say yes!" Quinn begged. "Say yes to a dress!"

She maneuvered captive Winston's paws into a begging position.

"Wait, why would we even have a playground wedding?" Claire asked.

"First and most important," Emma said, "you like Kevin. Yes or no?"

"Yes," Claire said. "But—"

"Second, you like weddings. Yes or no?"

"Yes," Claire said. "But—"

"Third, this could be huge for EmMatchmaker," Emma said. "HUGE. Isla's festival-planning meeting is Friday. If you have a wedding on Thursday and everyone goes, they've GOT to let me have a matchmaking booth."

"I want to do it," Claire said. "But—"

"What if Kevin says yes?" Emma asked. "If Kevin says yes, will you have a playground wedding?"

"If Kevin says yes"—Claire took a breath—"then I'll do it."

"Yay!" Quinn cheered out loud, holding Winston's paws up like he was raising the roof. "Wait a minute. Is this going to be at recess? Kindergartners have a different recess than fourth graders. How am I going to be flower girl? Can Mom write a note? Should I sneak out?"

As Quinn talked, Emma realized what she'd just taken on.

Emma had to plan a wedding. In two days.

And she wasn't even sure the "groom" would say yes.

CHAPTER 19

TO: EVERYONE IN FOURTH GRADE

You are invited to attend the

 Wedding of the School Year!

Claire + Kevin

WHERE: Playground—under the monkey bars

WHEN: Thursday at recess

Emma was so excited! But freaking out! But excited! Eee! The playground wedding was minutes away. Emma hoped she could pull this off. Students—no, *wedding guests*—were starting to gather at the monkey bars, waiting to see the ceremony.

Emma, Claire, and Rosemeen stood hidden behind the jungle gym, keeping Claire as much out of sight as they could from the other students and especially the groom. The playground monitors were suspicious and kept coming to check on them, but all they saw were two girls fussing over another one's hair.

"You look so pretty," Emma told Claire. Claire beamed. She was wearing a lacy white dress that she had promised her mom she wouldn't get dirty. Rosemeen had put a little flower barrette in her hair.

Annie had asked Henry to get flowers again—but this time for Claire's bouquet. It included:

✴ Orange and red marigolds from his mother's garden

✴ Yellow dandelions from the schoolyard

✴ White-seeded dandelions that you can blow and make a wish on. They looked a little scraggly because the wind had gotten to them.

Actually, all the flowers looked a little scraggly, because Claire was clutching the stems in a nervous death grip.

Emma was the maid of honor. As Claire's best friend, she would of course be by her side. But Emma also was running the show.

"I better go check on everything," Emma said. "Be right back."

Emma scanned the playground to make sure everything was in place. Then she checked on the other most important piece of this wedding: the groom. Kevin was standing with Henry over by the swings. Emma had asked Henry to keep an eye on him and prevent him from fleeing.

"Kevin," Emma said. "Everything cool?"

"Uh," Kevin said. "Uh."

Emma noticed he was a little shaky. She looked at Henry and he shrugged.

"Wedding jitters," Emma said authoritatively. "It's totally normal."

"So . . . uh . . . everyone's going to watch this?" Kevin asked. He ran his fingers around the collar of his white button-down shirt as if it were choking him. Emma had asked him to dress up a little bit, and he looked nice in the shirt and khaki pants and the black bow that Emma had plucked out of the hair of a protesting Rosemeen and pinned to Kevin as a bow tie.

When Emma had asked Kevin if he would take part in something at recess with Claire, he had said sure, if Claire wanted to. Emma could tell he really liked Claire. It had taken a little more convincing once he found out it was a wedding.

"Well, yeah," Emma said. "Remember I'd said it was like a group project, like a play? Plays have an audience. Your audience is the fourth grade."

"You said 'group project,' not 'entire-fourth-grade project,'" Kevin said. "I thought it would be four or five people. Look, even the playground monitors are watching. No way. I'm not going to do this. Henry, you do it."

Uh-oh. Emma needed to convince him. How? Bribery. She'd give him treats afterward.

"Kevin. What's your favorite food?" Emma asked.

"Lobster with garlic butter," he answered. "The special kind from Maine we get on our vacations."

Erg. Not helpful.

"What's your favorite snack?" Emma asked.

"Zucchini bread," he said.

Emma sighed. Seriously? He couldn't have said cupcakes or BBQ chips or something? Now she had to find zucchini bread?

"My mom's special recipe," he added.

Now she had to *make* zucchini bread?

"Give me the recipe and I'll make you a ton," Emma grouched. "There, will you do it now?"

"For vegetable bread? No way," he said, looking out at the playground. "I'm sorry, but I didn't understand what this all meant. This is kind of scary. I better go."

No! A runaway groom was not allowed! Emma thought fast. She remembered how she'd persuaded him to ask Claire to dance. She'd appealed to his nice-guy rep, and it had worked.

"Kevin," Emma said. "Claire and I have a chance at getting a booth at the Happy Frogs Fall Festival. That is huge for EmMatchmaking."

Emma pointed at her T-shirt, which she'd made the night before. It had an iron-on of her EmMatch-making logo on the front. On the back it said: I MAKE YOUR PERFECT MATCH! Emma dressed it up by wearing a peach flowy skirt and the silver flats she'd worn to her father's office picnic.

"Kevin," Emma said. "This wedding is really important to us. All you have to do is the teeny tiny thing of walking over there and saying a few words to Claire. That's it! Look. She's waiting for you. Everyone's waiting for you. Please don't let us down."

"I don't want to let anyone down," Kevin mumbled. "And I don't want to embarrass Claire. She's nice."

"She *is* nice," Emma said genuinely. "And so are you."

"Okay. I'll do it."

YES!

"Do. Not. Let. Him. Change. His. Mind," Emma whisper-ordered Henry. Emma ran back to Claire before anything else went wrong.

Emma noticed approvingly that everyone had lined up in place as she ran back to Claire, who was standing with . . . Quinn? And Daniel's sister Rachel? And . . . Daniel?

"Emma! I get to come to the wedding!" Quinn was bouncing up and down with excitement, her white tutu bouncing along with her. "Rachel's going to be a flower girl, too!"

"Quinn is letting me borrow her tiara." Rachel smiled, pointing to the crooked plastic crown on her head.

"Does your teacher know you're out here?" Emma asked.

"I volunteer in the kindergarten class at lunch sometimes," Daniel told her. "I told their teacher Quinn's sister was putting on a show that she shouldn't miss."

Huh.

"Here, take some of my flowers," Claire told the girls. "Thanks, Daniel. That was nice."

"Thxxxmmf," Emma mumbled. That was the best thanks she could give right now. She couldn't even think about Daniel, standing there out of breath after helping the little girls. Yeah. Anyway. Okay.

The first sounds of music rang through the air. Marshall was playing the song Emma had asked him to learn on his violin.

"Is that . . ." Claire cocked her head. "You have him playing a Jake LaDrake song?"

"It's 'Perfect Match'!" Emma said, since the way Marshall's violin was screeching, it might be hard to tell. "The perfect playground-wedding song."

And EmMatchmaker's theme song! She would play it at her own wedding. Wait, no, Jake would *sing* it to her at their wedding, duh!

THE CELEBRITY WEDDING OF

Jake LaDrake to Emma Emmets *

WHERE: THE MOST ROMANTIC BEACH NEAR HOLLYWOOD

WHEN: VERY SOON, ONCE HER PARENTS ALLOW HER TO START DATING

* *No paparazzi allowed*

(Although of course they'd take pictures from helicopters and then Jake and Emma would be plastered all over the magazines and they would complain about privacy but really Emma would think she looked super pretty in all the photos.)

Emma imagined Jake in his tuxedo, looking into her eyes, putting a huuuge diamond ring on her finger, and saying, "Emma, I do."

"Emma! What do I do?!"

Emma snapped back to reality as her fingers were practically pulled off by an overexcited Quinn.

"Yes! Okay! Time for the flower girls," Emma said. "Walk together and toss flower petals!"

Emma could hear an *awww* from the crowd when the two flower girls skipped and tossed flower petals along the path.

"Follow exactly three steps behind me," Emma reminded Claire. "And happy wedding!" Emma stood up straight and tall and started to walk down the aisle.

Well, it was really the concrete path to the monkey bars, but still. Emma grinned as everyone quieted down. Yup, practically the whole fourth grade seemed to be there. Sure, there were some kids playing basketball and a couple kids calling out rude things about weirdos and wedding dorks and how Jake LaDrake's song stunk (hey!!), but that was to be expected. Everyone knew you weren't really a big deal unless you had a few haters.

Emma would focus on the wedding! And everyone was focused on Emma as she walked toward where Kevin and Henry were waiting! Emma smiled a classy maid-of-honor smile. Annie, the official photographer, was taking pictures with her phone. When Emma walked past her, she made sure to point to her EmMatchmaking shirt logo. Leah and Otto stood near each other. Emma noted with satisfaction that Isla was in the front row, watching intently.

Emma walked up and stood next to best man Henry and in between the flower girls.

Then it was Claire's turn to walk down the aisle.

"Psst," Emma hissed to Marshall. "Wedding song."

Violinist Marshall quickly started playing: *Here comes the bride, da DA da da.*

Claire was beaming! Emma had never seen her look so happy! Yet also a little nervous as she walked past all the fourth graders, who were staring at her. Claire walked up to the front.

"Hi," she said to Kevin and giggled.

They all turned to face Noah. Noah's dad was a rabbi, so Noah was chosen as the marrying person.

"Okay, uh," Noah said. He looked down at the paper that Emma had written out for him.

"We are gathered here for the playground wedding," he said. "Of Claire Imogen Roth and Kevin Hubert—"

Noah looked up.

"Hubert?" he asked. "Huuuubert."

Everyone cracked up.

"Guys! Shush!" Emma waved everyone quiet. "Noah, move on."

"Kevin *Hubert* Jones. Put on the rings now."

That wasn't exactly how Emma had written the script, but Henry handed one ring pop to Claire and another one to Kevin.

"I wanted the watermelon one," Kevin pointed out.

Claire switched with him. They both put on the rings.

"Do you, Kevin, take Claire to be your recess wife, blah blah blah," Noah said. He looked at Emma.

"I do," Claire said.

"Okay," Kevin said.

"I now pronounce you married! Well, playground married, anyway," Noah announced.

Everyone cheered! Emma cheered the loudest. Woo! Emma noticed Isla cheering, too. And a few playground monitors! Quinn was twirling around, throwing petals.

Claire and Kevin were standing together and smiling! The playground wedding was a success!!!!

"Now what?" Henry asked.

"Next, the bride and groom celebrate on the zip line!" Emma yelled. "Oh, but wait! First, a message from Noah."

"Oh!" Noah looked back at his sheet. "This playground wedding was brought to you by our one and only EmMatchmaker."

CHAPTER 💘 20

After school on Friday, Emma stood atop EmMatchmaker HQ, looking through the telescope. She was watching the back door of the school, where everyone would file outside after the Fall Festival meeting.

"The playground wedding was awesome. They have to say yes to the booth," Emma said, for the tenth time, to Claire, who was sitting on the deck below her. "Don't they?"

Ever since Isla had brought up the idea of an EmMatchmaking booth, Emma had been thinking and thinking about it. She'd even dreamed about it. The dream actually featured an EmMatchmaking booth up on a stage with a blinking neon sign. And Jake LaDrake was there, singing his new hit song "Emma Emmets, the Greatest Matchmaker in the World Is Mine, All Mine."

Emma had woken up smiling, thinking of dream-Jake serenading her with lyrics like: "It's EMpossible to be without you!"

"I think they'll say yes," Claire said. Ever since she'd met Emma on the playground after school, she'd been pretty subdued. Emma thought that Claire would be more excited. After all, she had just been the center of attention of the entire grade. The bride in the famous playground wedding!

"So how cool is it that everyone was talking about the playground wedding?" Emma said. Claire didn't answer. She was staring at her phone.

"Claire?" Emma asked. "You okay?"

"Yeah," she said. "Well, no. Kevin hasn't texted me back."

"Well," Emma said. "Maybe he's at soccer or homework help or something."

"Maybe," Claire said, sounding worried. "I didn't really get to talk to him after the wedding."

Claire suddenly got a text. Her eyes lit up and then darkened.

"My mom says she's here." Claire sighed. "She'll wait for us."

Emma turned the telescope to the parking lot and waved to Claire's mother. When Emma turned the scope back, she saw the door to the school opening.

"People are coming out!" Emma said.

Out came a stream of kids, followed by teachers, and finally she spotted long, black hair, and yes, there she was.

"There's Isla!" Emma said, her stomach in knots.

She watched as Isla climbed up to the jungle gym as planned, to tell the results.

"Did we get a matchmaking booth?" Emma asked, holding her breath.

"Yes," Isla said. "We did!"

Emma and Claire squealed and jumped around. ☺ ☺ ☺ ! Isla played it a little more chill but sort of shuffled around with them.

"You have to meet with Mrs. G first to discuss it," Isla said. "She wants to set ground rules. She said that 'Romance is a borderline message to be sending,' but I reassured her that it was all very age appropriate."

Emma and Claire nodded. Their parents were always talking about whether things were inappropriate or age appropriate. Especially when it came to romance.

"EmMatchmaker will be age appropriate and awesome appropriate," Emma said, grinning.

"And I have other great news," Isla said.

"Really? What?" Emma asked.

"I think you're ready to make my match," Isla said. EEEEEEEEEEEEEEEEE!

"I can do that," Emma said, sounding calm and confident while her mind went berserk. She would need to find just the right fourth grader. Two boys already had confessed crushes on Isla, so they were two candidates, and—

"Before I tell you who it is, you have to swear secrecy," Isla said.

"Wait, you have someone picked out?" Claire asked. "Don't you want Emma to find your perfect match?"

"I already know who it is," Isla said. "I just want Emma to make it happen. But nobody knows who it is, so you have to swear you'll keep it secret."

"Not even your friends know?" Claire asked.

"No," Isla said. "I didn't want them to go blab about it and mess it up. I need a professional."

"EmMatchmaker is known for its professionalness and its confidentiality," Emma said, making that up on the spot. "We swear."

"Okay then. Matchmake me with Parker," Isla said.

Parker? Emma couldn't think of any Parkers in fourth grade. There was a Peyton, a Peter, and a Porter, but no Parker.

"He's not in our grade," Isla said.

There was a Parker in fifth grade? She couldn't think of one. Wait, there was a Parker on her street—

"Parker in third grade?" Emma gasped.

"Ew! Not a third grader!" Isla looked horrified. "Parker Clark. The sixth grader."

Now Emma really gasped. And Claire gasped as well. Isla wanted a *sixth grader* as her boyfriend? Whoa. Emma had thought it was a big whoa when

Isla sat with *fifth* graders on the bus. A sixth grader. And she wanted Emma to make it happen. Urrrgh.

"He doesn't even go to school in our building," Emma tried. "I don't think I can get to the middle school. . . ."

"He has lacrosse practice after school," Isla said, pointing. "The fifth- and sixth-grade teams play right there on the ball fields."

Her eyes had a dreamy, faraway look to them.

"We had coed drills the other day, and he was on my team," Isla said. "He's so cute, running down the field, even with his mouthguard in."

"Wait, you're on the 5–6 team?" Emma asked.

"I play up," Isla said. "I'm really good."

Of course she was.

"Wouldn't you rather start with a fourth grader? I know at least two people who have big crushes on you. I could match you with either of them in two seconds," Emma said. Emma also knew about two hundred people who had crushes on Parker Clark. He was not only awesome at lacrosse but had starred in the school play last spring, and girls were lined up asking for his autograph after.

Plus, he was beyond cute.

"I can match myself with a fourth grader in one second," Isla said, crossing her arms. "Do you think I need to come to you for help with a fourth grader? Maybe it was a mistake to come to you at all."

"No, no, I can do it!" Emma protested. "Parker Clark! Yup, I got it. No problemo. Just keep in mind that it might take a little longer, since it's a sixth grader and all."

"I understand," Isla said. "But it can't take too long. We need to be dating by the Fall Festival so we can go together. Last year my sister Paloma went with her boyfriend. They're in seventh grade. He won her a goldfish by throwing a ping-pong ball in a cup. She named it after him. It's still alive. It was so romantic."

"Then I'll make it happen," Emma said. "You can count on EmMatchmaker."

"Maybe I underestimated you, Emma Emmets," Isla nodded.

"Maybe you did. I guess I'm not just a brown M&M," Emma said.

"A what?"

"A brown M&M?" Emma said. "You know, like you called me in first grade."

"I did?" Isla laughed.

"Yes." Emma was stunned. "You don't remember? You said I was like a brown M&M because I was like poo?"

"That's funny." Isla chuckled.

Emma gave a weak laugh. Oh ha-ha.

"Anyway," Emma said. "I have a new nickname now: EmMatchmaker."

And if Emma could matchmake a fourth grader with a sixth grader, she would earn that nickname for sure.

QUIZ: What Kind of Class Couple Would You Be?

Choose the class you'd most like to share with him:

- ✱ English: Sigh! You're pure romantics!
- ✱ Science: You have great chemistry together!
- ✱ Math: Could "add up" to something great!
- ✱ PE: Sporty, spunky, and something to cheer about!
- ✱ Lunch: Sweet and satisfying!

CHAPTER ❤ 21

"A *sixth grader?* Do sixth graders even date fourth graders? *Should* sixth graders even date fourth graders? Should sixth graders even *talk* to fourth graders?" Claire shriek-freaked.

Emma and Claire were on the teeter-totter, after Isla had left the playground to go to lacrosse practice.

"I know," Emma said grimly. "It's a challenge. But we have to solve it. Think of the payoff: everyone knowing I fixed up Isla Cruz. With her perfect match."

"I know you're a genuine, gifted matchmaker," Claire said. "But this one seems hopeless."

"I can't think like that," Emma said. "We have to stay positive. Things are going great. The booth, now this."

Hmm. So far, Emma had chosen matches for people. She'd picked people she thought would like each other, had things in common, or could make a winning leapfrog team. But this was a different game altogether. Emma hoped Parker and Isla had things in common. Like Emma and Jake LaDrake did.

Jake LaDrake	Emma
Likes to play guitar and ukulele	Likes to listen to the guitar and thinks the ukulele is interesting
Loves spaghetti with meatballs	Loves spaghetti! Except with no meatballs and no sauce either, just butter
Favorite drink is lemonade	Doesn't like lemonade but doesn't think it's a deal breaker
Favorite subjects are math and music	Has two favorite subjects too! (Not math and music. Science and reading. But still.)
Has a cat named Fred	Has a cat named Winston!!!

"I've got to find out more about Parker Clark," Emma said. "But how?"

"Who has a sister or brother in sixth grade?" Claire asked.

"Rosemeen," Emma said. But she didn't want to ask anyone besides Claire for help. Especially not chatty Rosemeen. If people were to believe she had a superpower, she needed to be stealth.

Be stealth. That was it! That's what she needed to do!

"We need to spy," Emma said. "We need to watch Parker Clark and find out more about him. Then, we share what we find out with Isla."

And then, Emma explained, she would tell Isla what they found and figure out what matched between then. Then she would make a plan to get Isla to talk to Parker, and he would see how much they had in common. And a perfect match would be made!

"Okay," Claire said, looking doubtful. "You're the expert."

"I bet if we hurry, we can get over to the middle school and check him out now," Emma said.

"Okay," Claire said, pulling out her phone. She sighed. "It's not like I have anything else to do."

"Still nothing from Kevin?" Emma asked. Claire shook her head, sadly.

QUIZ: Is Your Relationship on the Rocks?

* Has (s)he stopped returning your
   texts or calls?
* Does (s)he pay less attention
   to you?
* Does (s)he make excuses not
   to see you?

If you answered more than one yes, these might be clues. Ask the other person if they still want to be more than friends. But be prepared—you may not want to hear the answer. But knowing the truth will be far less painful and embarrassing in the long run.

Claire's mom drove them the short distance to the middle school, and they waited until school was letting out. Emma and Claire got out of the minivan and headed to the front of the middle school as the older students poured out of the building, yelling and screaming.

"Oof," Claire said as a mob pushed by them to get to their buses or their parents' cars or their after-school activities.

Emma spotted shaggy black hair and a maroon-and-gold lacrosse uniform shirt with a number 23 on it. It was Parker Clark!

"I see him!" Emma said and steered Claire through the crowd toward Parker. He was walking with a few boys and girls down the sidewalk, then across the lawn.

"He's probably going to go to lacrosse," Emma said. "Tell your mom we're on the move."

"You do know this is kind of weird," Claire said. "Right?"

"Shh." Emma grinned. "Just be stealth."

Emma pictured herself as Secret Agent Emma Emmets in dark sunglasses and a trench coat following a target. Emma made fake conversation as they followed Parker and his friends across the lawn. Then he took an unexpected detour from the athletic fields.

"Maybe there's no practice today," Emma said. "Is he walking home?"

Emma and Claire oh-so-subtly followed Parker

and his friends down the sidewalk, as Claire's mom trailed behind them in her car.

"Ah." Emma realized where they were going. "They're going to get fro yo."

A lot of middle schoolers went to the frozen yogurt place after school. Emma and Claire walked up the path until they reached the little plaza. A red-and-white-striped sign welcomed them to YO! FroYO.

"Oh, goody," Claire said. "I'm hungry."

"We can't just walk in there," Emma said. "He'll see us. We have to spy."

Emma waited until Parker and his friends were inside. She crouched down and peeked through the large front window. Claire sat down on the ground next to her.

"Lay low," Emma told Claire. "I'll tell you what's going on."

Emma gave the play-by-play in a hushed, spylike voice.

"Parker's pulling out his phone," Emma continued. "It has a black-and-red cover. Since Parker is also wearing black sneakers with a red swoosh, I'm guessing he likes black and red."

See? Emma had already found out something important.

"Parker is ordering frozen yogurt," Emma said. "It looks like cake batter?"

"Now I'm really hungry," Claire said. "Can you see the board? What are today's flavors?"

Emma read them off to her:

Frozen Yogurt Flavors

* ✳ Vanilla
* ✳ Chocolate
* ✳ Strawberry
* ✳ Cake batter
* ✳ Peanut butter
* ✳ Red velvet
* ✳ Mint chocolate
* ✳ Pomegranate

"I want peanut butter," Claire moaned. "With cookie crumbles and chocolate syrup."

"Wait! The target is ordering toppings," Emma continued her report. "An unusual choice for cake batter. Swedish Fish."

"Yum, Swedish Fish," Daniel said.

"I know," Emma agreed with him.

Wait. Agreed with *who*? Emma and Claire both turned around and shriek-freaked. Daniel was standing right behind them. He was wearing a bright T-shirt with a California college logo on it, long plaid shorts, and flip-flops.

His little sister was nearby on the sidewalk, cracking up.

"Ha! You were right! You scared them!" Rachel called out.

"He didn't scare us," Emma said. "Surprising is different from scaring."

"You guys were like, 'Eeek!'" Rachel continued cracking up so hard, the weight of her lavender backpack almost tipped her over backward.

"Heh," Daniel said. "That was hilarious. Why are you guys spying on the Swedish Fish?"

"We're not spying on the Swedish Fish." Emma rolled her eyes.

"We're spying on Parker Clark," Claire blurted out.

"Claire!" Emma nudged her. "Shh!"

"Who's spying?" Rachel asked. "Is it for another wedding? Can I be a flower girl again? That was so cool!"

"Rachel, how about you go inside and buy our frozen yogurt," Daniel said, holding out some money.

"But—"

"You can get *two* toppings," he said. Rachel took the money and skipped inside.

"Okay, fine, we're spying on Parker Clark," Emma said.

Daniel shrugged. "I have no idea who that is."

"He's a sixth grader, black haired, and a lacrosse player." Emma sighed. "He likes cake-batter frozen yogurt, Swedish Fish, and the colors black and red. And he is notoriously cute."

"Uh, okay," Daniel said. "TMI. Too much information."

"FYI, I know what TMI means." Emma rolled her eyes. "And I need to get even more 'I' about Parker Clark."

"Do you want me to ask him something?" Daniel asked.

"Really?" Claire asked. "That would be great! Tell him what to ask, Emma."

"Well, I want to know what he likes," Emma said. "His favorite foods and things to do and stuff like that."

"Why do you want to know that?" Daniel asked. "Wait, I don't want to know. I'll be right back."

Emma was suspicious. Why was Daniel being so nice to her? First, he had helped out by getting the girls to the playground wedding. Now, he was helping her get info for her matchmaking? And was it her imagination, or did he seem a little jealous when she'd said Parker was cute? Maybe Daniel thought *she* liked Parker.

Her superpower started to tingle. Or whatever a superpower would do when it's going into action.

Did Daniel have a crush on her?

Emma had maybe thought that before in gym class. But now she really thought it. It would make perfect sense. Whoa. Emma could try to get one question from her "Is It a Crush?" quiz answered now:

Do your friends notice when you act
crushy around this person?

"Claire," Emma said quietly. "Do you think Daniel acts a certain way around me? Like he might . . . maybe . . . do you think . . . Daniel might like me?"

Emma looked to Claire for a response. She was looking at her phone.

"Claire?" Emma asked.

"Yay! It's Kevin! Kevin texted me," Claire squealed. "Yay! Sorry, what did you say?"

"Nothing," Emma said. "Forget it. And yay for Kevin! What did he say?"

"He said he turned off his cell because he was getting too many texts from people about the wedding," Claire said. Then she frowned. "Making fun of him."

Uh-oh.

QUIZ: Which Amusement-Park Ride Describes
You and Your Crush?

A) Rollercoaster: Has its ups and downs

B) Teacups: Makes you dizzy

C) Bumper cars: A bumpy ride

D) Merry-go-round: Same thing over and
over and over

E) Ferris wheel: Makes you feel on top
of the world

"I feel like this is my fault. The wedding was my idea," Emma said. "I'll talk to him for you if you want."

"Now he said he has to go. I don't have a good feeling about this," Claire said quietly.

Emma thought about it.

* Has (s)he stopped returning your
texts or calls?

✻ Does (s)he make excuses not
to see you?

Yes to both? Uh-oh. They didn't have a chance to discuss it further. Daniel came out of the frozen yogurt store, Rachel in tow.

"Parker Clark likes lacrosse, video games, paintball, lasagna, and flaming-hot cheese puffs," Daniel said. Then he listed Parker's favorite band and favorite movie.

Emma and Claire looked at each other.

"Wow," Emma said. "How did you find all that out?"

"I told him that the girl spying on him in the window wanted to know his deepest, darkest thoughts," Daniel said. "And she thought he was notoriously cute."

"WHAT?!" Emma yelped.

"I'm kidding!" Daniel said. "I told him I was trying out for the school newspaper and needed a story about an athlete."

"Oh! Okay," Emma said. "Huh. That's pretty clever."

"I'm a clever guy," Daniel preened. "Plus it's true, because I am trying out for the school newspaper and need a story. It's not going to be about him, but since I didn't say that, I wasn't lying."

"That's awesome," Emma said.

"Yup, I'm awesome," Daniel said. "Here's his cell number in case you need more."

Emma was not even annoyed by this. She was actually really impressed. Daniel might be kind of obnoxious and have a big ego. But he also got things done. She liked that. Yup, she liked that quite a bit.

Wait.

Emma suddenly felt like it was hard to concentrate. She felt her cheeks turning red. She suddenly felt nervous. She thought about her crush quiz:

1. *Do you feel nervous when you're around this person?*

3. *Do you have trouble concentrating when this person is around?*

4. *Do you blush when this person is mentioned?*

Yes to numbers 1, 3, and 4 all at once? Did she *like...* him?

EE + DD = ??? !!!! ????

"Yup," Emma stammered.

"Did you just say 'yup,' that I'm awesome?" Daniel said. "Yes! Now say I'm awesome and the best line leader and can beat you in every trivia question."

"Nope," Emma said. "No way."

That was pushing it.

CHAPTER ♥ 22

"Who knew there were so many crushes in fourth grade?" Emma muttered to Winston. She was sitting at her white desk, where she had put her mom's laptop.

Winston was sitting on the desktop, occasionally batting at Emma's fingers as she typed. Emma had taken a quiz in her magazine:

QUIZ: *Are You Crush Crazy?*

- *Do you think about your crush more than practically anything else?*

- *Do you focus on your crush more than your friends?*

- *Does thinking about your crush distract you from your schoolwork?*

- *Do your friends tell you that you're too obsessed with your crush?*

If you answered yes to, well, any of these questions, you may be too CRUSH CRAY-CRAY. Make sure you take time to focus on your family, schoolwork, friends, and extra-curricular activities!

Emma would answer that at least one-third of the fourth grade was crush CRAY-CRAY! She had made a spreadsheet on the computer to keep track of EmMatchmaking.

MATCHED

Annie——Otto

Claire——Kevin

Violet——Aiden

The boy who liked the girl with red hair——the ginger girl

The girl who made desserts——the boy who ate them

She typed in a few more people in the IN PROGRESS column. There was the boy looking for a science-lab partner. The girl who just wanted her forever-crush to talk to her one time. Isla and Parker Clark (fingers crossed!).

Emma paused. Maybe her and Daniel? Maybe? Maybe not. Maybe. Maybe yes. Eeee! After Daniel had gotten the information about Parker Clark, he and Rachel had taken their frozen yogurt and left. Daniel had gotten vanilla with rainbow sprinkles.

"Just like you, Jake," Emma said to her cardboard cutout of Jake LaDrake. She had seen a picture in a magazine of Jake eating a cone with rainbow sprinkles. Personally, Emma preferred chocolate sprinkles, but she didn't think that was a deal breaker.

Emma shook her head to clear it. Emma couldn't waste time thinking about Daniel. She had to focus on EmMatchmaking.

"Knock knock," Mom said as she poked her head through the door.

"Wow, you and Winston are really working hard on that project." Mom came into Emma's room. "Is it for English class?"

"No," Emma said. "It's actually not for school. It's . . ."

Emma's voice trailed off. She remembered the conversation she'd had with her parents where they weren't so happy about matchmaking. She wanted her parents to be excited for this.

"I have great news!" Emma said brightly. "I was asked to have my own booth at the Happy Frogs Fall Festival!"

"Really? That's wonderful!" Mom said. "What an honor. What kind of booth?"

Emma explained EmMatchmaking to her mom.

"Hmm," her mom said. "I can see the appeal. But isn't this a bit tricky? I'm not sure romance at your age is always a good idea."

"Mom," Emma said. "Two words: David Michaels."

Mom got a dreamy look on her face. David Michaels had been her elementary school crush. She even still kept a Valentine's Day card he'd given to her.

Be my valentine!

You're groovy! Let's boogie!

Luv, David

"He was cute," Mom admitted. "I remember when we won the disco dance competition together in gym class. . . ."

Emma had heard this story at least a thousand times before, but she wasn't going to cut off her mom. It was helping her make the point.

"See?" Emma said, when her mom had finished the story (with the exciting! moment! when her dancing opponents tripped over their wide-legged pant fringe and fell). "Even *you* had a match. Imagine if I could help other people with their crushes!"

"I suppose crushes are normal at this age for some boys and girls," Mom said.

"Some people think it's gross," Emma said. "So it's only for people who are into it. We're making matches for science-lab partners. Gym-class dance partners. Stuff like that, too."

"That sounds respectful," her mother said. "There will be adult supervision?"

Emma nodded.

"Did I ever show you the valentine that David sent me?" Mom asked. "I have it somewhere. . . ."

A ding sounded; Emma had an alert on the computer. She pressed a button and Claire's face popped up on the screen.

"Mom, you go find it and I'll talk to Claire?" Emma suggested, then turned to face the computer. "Hi. I just told my mom about the booth. She's cool with it."

"Good," Claire said. "Hi, Winston!"

Winston had pushed his face up against the computer screen. He plumped down on the keyboard.

"Winston says 'aksq2n;asgh,'" Emma said, reading from the screen. Winston protested as Emma gently moved him off to the side. He sat, offended, licking his paws and rubbing them on his face.

"So how are things with Kevin?" Emma asked hesitantly.

"Better," Claire said. "He was . . . well, he said the wedding thing was kind of crazy. He thought we were doing a small class project kind of thing, not the whole grade."

"Oh," Emma said. Um. Oops.

"But I told him how it helped you out and also, well . . ." Claire paused. "I told him I really like him. And he said he liked me, too! And then I helped him with our math homework. So everything is okay."

"Whew," Emma said. "That's good."

"He's texting me now!" Claire squealed. "Gotta go!" Claire's face disappeared.

Emma got up and turned on "The Perfect Match" on her iPod.

"You're my perfect match," Emma sang along with Jake. "The perfect match for meeee!"

She danced around Cardboard Jake. He was a much better partner than Coach. She spun him around and dipped him.

Emma was so enthralled with Cardboard Jake that she didn't hear her door swing open. She didn't know that Quinn had entered, just as Emma was in mid-dip with Jake.

"Winston!" Quinn cooed, surprising her. She reached down and grabbed him around his big belly and hoisted him up. Winston wriggled in Quinn's arms and tried to escape. Winston desperately wanted to bolt, and Emma felt the same way.

Because someone else followed Quinn into Emma's room.

CHAPTER ♥ 23

If Emma had known beforehand that Isla Cruz was going to walk into her room, she wouldn't have been swing dancing with Cardboard Jake. While singing loudly.

Erg!!

"Look! My friend came for a playdate," Quinn said, pointing to Isla. "Winston, this is Isla. Isla, do you want to play Pollys? Do you want to play dress up? I'll let you wear my new mermaid costume. Or my zombie one that drips fake blood."

"You're so cute," Isla cooed. "But I need to talk to your sister, okay?"

"But—" Quinn started to protest. Winston sensed a moment and wriggled free. Then he leaped to the ground and attached himself to Isla's jeans. He dangled from Isla's leg.

"Yow!" Isla yelled. "Yow yow yowch!"

"Winston," Emma said as she ran up and detached Winston from Isla's leg. Winston suddenly spazzed out. He clawed at Emma's curtains, jumped down onto her pink furry round chair, and zoomed under Quinn's legs and out the door.

"Your cat is crazy!" Isla shuddered.

"Yup," Quinn said proudly.

"Quinn, out," Emma directed. "Isla, hi. I wasn't expecting you."

"Well, you texted me that you had information," Isla said. "It sounded important, so I thought we should talk privately."

Isla looked around Emma's room. Emma felt awkward and wished she could have closed her undies drawer and not left her stuffed animals in pairs, dancing around the floor of her room.

"You have a Jake LaDrake?" Isla said. "I used to think he was so cute. My parents asked me if I wanted to go to his concert up north, but I'm so over him."

Emma sighed as she swept some things off her bed and then kicked them underneath.

"Have a seat," Emma said.

Isla smoothed the surface of the bed and then sat down on the purple comforter. In her cream sweater, skinny red jeans, and brown boots, she looked just like a model, posing.

"Here's what I found out," Emma said. "Parker Clark likes lacrosse, video games, paintball, lasagna, and flaming-hot cheese puffs."

"Nice," Isla nodded.

"And cake-batter frozen yogurt with Swedish Fish," Emma said. Then she rattled off the names of his favorite band and movie.

"Impressive," Isla said. "You do know what you're doing."

"Yup." Emma nodded. "And I know what *you* need to do next."

Emma had asked Daniel to text Parker to meet again at the frozen yogurt store to interview more after lacrosse practice. Emma had agreed to buy Daniel frozen yogurt (vanilla with rainbow sprinkles!) if he did.

CHAPTER 24

WHAT WAS SUPPOSED TO HAPPEN:

PHASE ONE:

* Isla was to meet up with Parker as he walked to lacrosse after school.
* She would happen to have flaming-hot cheese puffs to share.
* Her ringtone would go off—a new song by Parker's favorite band that Emma downloaded for her. They would talk about the band.
* Isla would tell him about her basement, which had a huge TV and three different video-game consoles and surround-sound game chairs. (That part was Isla's idea. Emma thought it was kind of braggy but effective.)
* Bonus points if she could throw in comments about paintball.

PHASE TWO:

* Isla would run to the frozen yogurt store after lacrosse practice.

✱ Emma would "run into" Parker and set up the match.

PHASE THREE:

✱ Isla and Parker would eat frozen yogurt together!

✱ Isla would Isla-charm Parker!

✱ A match would be made!

WHAT REALLY HAPPENED:

✱ Phase 1 worked exactly as planned! This turned out to be deceptive.

✱ Phase 2 also went according to plan. Emma waited for Isla's text and then "accidentally" bumped into Parker.

"Hey," Emma said. Actually, more like panted because she had to run to catch up with Parker and his friends, who walked seriously fast. "Are you going to the frozen yogurt place?"

"Uh, yeah?" Parker asked. "Who are you?"

Oops. Emma flushed purplish red. Emma had been watching Parker for twenty-four hours and felt like she already knew him. Except, of course, he didn't know her at all.

"You know the guy who interviewed you for the newspaper? I'm with him," Emma explained. "I mean, not *with* him. We're not together, heh, or anything like *that*."

Parker made a face like she might be crazy. He looked around for a way to escape, similar to the way

Winston looked whenever Quinn came in the room.

"Look, I'm helping with his project," Emma said. "Can I talk to you in private for a second?"

Parker shrugged. "I guess." His friends scattered.

"Want some Swedish Fish?" Emma pulled out a bag. Parker took a few.

"So. Parker Clark. You know the girl who talked to you on the way to lacrosse? Isla?" Emma asked. "Isn't she nice?"

Parker had to think for a minute.

"Sure, she gave me some flaming-hot cheese puffs," he said.

They walked up the hill to the path leading to the frozen yogurt place. Parker was walking so fast, Emma felt like she might run out of time. And breath.

"You should see her game room," Emma said. "It's got every video game you can imagine and a projection screen and surround-sound game chairs."

"Cool," Parker said.

"She's really pretty, too," Emma said.

"Yeah," he said. They reached the parking lot of the frozen yogurt place. Emma could see Isla waiting out front for her, dressed to impress in a blue denim dress, tall boots, and her hair up in a sophisticated messy bun. Okay. This was it!

"You like paintball, right? Do you think you would want to play paintball with her?" Emma said.

"Yeah," Parker said.

YEAH! Parker said yeah! Emma gave a silent cheer. They were close enough to Isla for Emma to give a thumbs-up to her. Isla grinned and clapped her hands together.

It was time for Emma to make this match!

"So, it's safe to say you like her?" Emma asked.

"Wait, what?" Parker said.

"You like Isla?" Emma asked.

"I thought you asked if I like paintball." Parker stopped walking. "Not a girl."

"Uh, you said she's pretty and nice and you'd play paintball with her," Emma said. "Right?"

Please say right.

"I didn't say I *liked* her liked her," Parker said. "Why would I like her?"

Uh-oh. Isla was walking toward them with a smile on her face.

"Why wouldn't you like her?" Emma said. "All the boys like her. She's the most popular girl in fourth grade."

"Fourth grade?" Parker said. "I'm in *sixth* grade. I'm not going to *like* like someone in *fourth grade*!"

"Uh," Emma said. "Isla plays on the 5–6 lacrosse team!"

"Uh, she's still in *fourth grade*," Parker said. "Dude. No way!"

Uh-oh! Uh-oh! Emma started to frantically wave to Isla to stop walking toward them. She shook her head no. She made slicing motions at her neck.

EMergency! EMergency! Go back, Isla! Go back!

But apparently Isla only had eyes for Parker. She got closer and closer.

"What if I give you Swedish Fish every day for a month and bring you lasagna and cake-batter frozen yogurt?" Emma was getting desperate. "I'll host a paintball party just for you!"

"This is getting seriously weird," Parker said, walking faster.

"Look," Emma said. "Can you just roll with this for, like, a day or so? Isla really likes you and I have this whole matchmaking thing going and a booth at the Fall Festival and you don't have to date but maybe you could just go get frozen yogurt with her? Anything? Please?"

Emma panted, completely out of breath. And full of shame.

"No," Parker said. "No fourth graders is one reason. And there's another reason."

"What?" Emma asked.

Emma followed his gaze. A girl with long curly brown hair was walking toward them from the other direction.

"That's my girlfriend," Parker said.

CHAPTER ✏️ 25

His *girlfriend*?!?!?!?

Why didn't Isla tell her that Parker Clark had a girlfriend? Why didn't Daniel "I Can Find Out Anything" Dunne find out he had a girlfriend?!! A girlfriend who was walking toward them at the exact time his "perfect match" Isla was?!

"Hiiiii!" The girl bounced up to them.

"Hiiiii!" Isla bounced up to them at the same time. She held out a bag. "Anyone want some Swedish Fish?"

"What is with the Swedish Fish?" Parker groaned.

"Okay, see you, we have to go." Emma tried to steer Isla away.

"We're going to get frozen yogurt, right, Parker?" Isla was not getting the hint.

"Hi, who are you?" Parker's GIRLFRIEND asked Isla.

"I'm Isla, who are you?" Isla asked.

"I'm Tallulah. Parker's *girlfriend*," the girl said.

"Well, I'm . . ." Isla's voice trailed off. She flashed Emma a look of confusion that quickly morphed to fury, then changed back to a fake smile.

"Here to get Emma for frozen yogurt," Isla said. "So, let's go, Emma."

Isla grabbed Emma's arm and steered her quickly away from the couple and in the other direction. As they walked away, they could hear Tallulah ask Parker: "Why did she say she was getting frozen yogurt with you?"

"I don't know. Fourth graders are weird," Parker answered.

"If they're getting fro yo, why are they walking away from the frozen yogurt place?"

"I don't know," Parker answered.

"Just. Keep. Walking," Isla said through gritted teeth.

They hid behind the Dumpster next to the frozen yogurt place. Isla turned to Emma.

"Oops?" Emma said meekly.

"Why didn't you tell me Parker Clark had a girlfriend?" Isla hissed. "That was so humiliating!"

"I didn't know!" Emma said. "I kind of thought since you were after him, you knew he was single."

"Isn't that your job, to figure those things out? Aren't you EmMatchmaker?" Isla asked.

"Well," Emma said, getting a little bit annoyed. "As EmMatchmaker, I usually use my talent to choose the perfect match. You went ahead and picked yours— *not me*. So this actually doesn't reflect on EmMatchmaking at all."

There. That sounded persuasive.

"I hear frozen yogurt's good when you get dumped," Emma suggested, waving toward the frozen yogurt place.

"I wasn't dumped," Isla growled. "You can't be dumped by someone who already has a girlfriend."

"You have a point," Emma agreed.

"I want strawberry," Isla grumbled. "With mini chocolate chips."

QUIZ: Is Your Crush Worth It?

Keep or Dump?

Is your crush:

☐ Sweet like candy?

☐ A rude dude?

Does your crush:

☐ Make you laugh?

☐ Make you cry?

Will your crush:

☐ Be there for you?

☐ Be somewhere else?

Will your crush:

☐ Treat you right?

☐ Start a fight?

Emma thought this quiz needed another question:

Does your crush:

☐ ALREADY HAVE A GIRLFRIEND?

Isla's cell phone went off. "Oh great, everyone is texting to ask how it went with my new boyfriend."

"What are you going to tell them?" Emma said.

"I don't know yet," Isla said. "The good news is that I didn't tell anyone who my mystery boyfriend was. Thank goodness."

"So? Did it work?" Daniel suddenly appeared from behind the Dumpster.

"Yeesh, Emma, did *you* tell everyone?" Isla asked. "What happened to client confidentiality?"

Emma shot Daniel a look.

"Uh," Daniel said. "It's not like that. I was an official assistant on this job. I signed a confidentiality agreement and am sworn to secrecy."

Emma had to give it to Daniel. That did sound professional.

"And it was the assistant's job to extract information," Emma pointed out. "So in a way, it's kind of his fault."

"For your information, Emma Emmets just humiliated me," Isla accused. "She tried to matchmake me with someone who has a *girlfriend*."

"Parker Clark," Emma said.

"Ohhhh," Daniel said. "Is that why you needed that information?"

"Well, yeah," Emma said. "Why else would I want to know that he ate lasagna?"

Daniel shrugged. "I thought *you* liked him."

"You liked Parker?" Isla turned to Emma. "Were you copying me? Did you sabotage my crush on purpose?"

"What?" Emma said. "No!"

"It was humiliating," Isla repeated, amping up the drama. "His girlfriend was like, who are *you*? *I'm* his girlfriend, so back off!"

"If it makes you feel any better, he was weirded out that you were in fourth grade," Emma said. "So he wouldn't have dated you even if he didn't already have Tallulah."

"You tried to matchmake a fourth grader with a sixth grader who had a girlfriend?" Daniel laughed. "HA! What part of that seemed like a good idea?"

"Oh, be quiet," Emma and Isla both snapped at him.

"EmMatchmaking was an epic FAIL," Isla announced. Then she lowered her voice and leaned in so only Emma could hear. "I should have known you would screw this up, B. Em."

"There she is! Isla!" a voice squealed, interrupting them as they glared at each other. Isla's friends descended like a plague of locusts surrounding their queen.

"Isla, is this your boyfriend?" one of the friends said. "You're right! He's really cute!"

"Wha?" Daniel backed away and slunk around the corner.

"Guys!" Isla said to her friends. "Just shush! Come with me. Now!"

Isla marched off, followed by her people. Emma exhaled and leaned against the wall.

Buzz! Emma looked at her cell phone.

> **IslaCruz**: Forget about the matchmaking booth! EmMatchmaking is OVER!

Emma was left alone, by herself, her matchmaking dreams in shambles. She slumped against the wall with her eyes closed. EmMatchmaking an epic fail? No matchmaking booth? How could this have gone so wrong?

"You have to admit, it's a little funny," Daniel said, popping back from around the corner. "Plus, some girl called me cute."

Emma's eyes snapped open.

"Grrr," she grumbled. "You're still here? Well, I'm so glad we entertained you with our embarrassment and our heartbreak."

"Heartbreak, psh," Daniel said. "They didn't know each other. That guy didn't even know who Isla was. That's not heartbreak. That's just rejection."

"I actually meant *my* heartbreak that I can't have my EmMatchmaking booth," Emma said.

"Oh," Daniel said. "Sorry."

"Flaming-hot cheese puffs, paintball . . . you couldn't have found out the guy had a girlfriend?" Emma asked.

"You didn't exactly tell me what you were looking for when I volunteered to help you out of the goodness of my heart," Daniel said.

"You're right." Emma sighed. "So, wait, you thought *I* liked Parker?"

Was it her imagination or did Daniel get a little squirmy?

"But you still helped me?" Emma said. "Also, why are you suddenly helping me?"

"I didn't say I was helping you," Daniel said. "I was merely proving I was superior because I could get the information you couldn't."

"So I guess you enjoyed watching this," Emma grumbled. "The epic fail of EmMatchmaking. It's all destroyed. My booth will be canceled. Nobody's going to come to me now."

"Oh, come on, this won't ruin everything," Daniel said. "It's just one person."

"One person who is the most popular girl in school," Emma said. "The one who got me my very own matchmaking booth in the first place. She's probably going to cancel it now!"

"Whoa, you really want this matchmaking booth, don't you?" Daniel said.

"Yes," Emma wailed. "You don't know anything because you're new, but the Happy Frogs Fall Festival is *huge. Everyone* goes."

"Well, make sure Isla doesn't screw it up for you," Daniel said. "Make it so she can't resist. It looked like she wasn't going to tell anyone what really happened."

"That's true," Emma admitted. "She's probably thinking of a new story right now so she doesn't look embarrassed. But she texted me that EmMatchmaking is OVER. So she's going to ruin my reputation somehow."

"Maybe it's not too late," he said. "You wanted EmMatchmaker to make a high-profile match, right? One that everyone talked about, right?"

"Right," Emma said.

"What if you still made a match today?" Daniel said. "Just not Isla and Parker?"

Emma didn't get it at first. But then Daniel pointed to himself.

Himself. Daniel?

Hey. Maybe he was right! If she made Isla a match even before Isla could tell people what had happened, everything would go forward exactly as planned! It wouldn't be with Parker Clark, but . . .

Isla's friends had already seen her with Daniel! They thought he was her new boyfriend! And they said he was CUTE!

"This actually could work." Emma gasped. "But why would you do it?"

"For the cause, to save your whole reputation. And because I'm awesome," Daniel said. "I mean, I'm not looking for a girlfriend. But we're both smart and good-looking people, so ha, why not? Plus it could be kind of fun to go to the Fall Festival or whatever. Things like that."

Whoa.

Daniel was willing to get matchmade with Isla.

Actually, Daniel seemed more than willing. Daniel was smiling. He was actually happy about it? Well, duh. Of course he was. Isla was super pretty and super popular and blah blah blooey. (And apparently Daniel also thought she was smart.)

Who wouldn't like Isla?

Emma felt a pang in her heart. She had thought Daniel maybe liked her. Maybe she'd liked him back. Now he was suggesting she match him up with Isla.

Daniel + . . . Isla?

"You're leaving me hanging here. You need to do this fast, right?" Daniel said. "Put the word out there before Isla ruins your matchmaking thing?"

"True," Emma admitted. "The faster we take care of this the better. But . . ."

Emma took a deep breath to say yes. But then she closed it. Then she opened her mouth to say something different. She was going to say no. She would tell him that *she* liked him and Isla couldn't have him. Emma opened her mouth.

And that was when Daniel spoke.

"Look, if you don't want to do this, just say so," Daniel said. "But you have to admit, it makes sense. I think we should just do it."

Emma closed her mouth. Daniel was blushing. Did he have a crush on *Isla?*

Do you blush when this person is mentioned?

Aggggh! Obviously, he was all into the possibility of Isla being his girlfriend. Well, fine. Isla could have him. If she even wanted him. Who knew if she'd even say yes? Daniel was acting like it was a done deal. Like no one would ever turn him down. He was seriously arrogant.

Emma scowled. "Fine. Let's do it."

Well. So. That was that. At least she would have a chance to save EmMatchmaker. That was most important . . . right?

QUIZ: **Which Kind of Movie Is Your Relationship Most Like?**

A) An action-adventure: Exciting! Filled with thrills!

B) Rom-com: Part romance, part laugh-out-loud funny

C) Sci-fi: Out of this world!

D) Horror: Frightening with weird creatures

E) G-rated: Age appropriate and parent approved

Unfortunately, Emma would now have to watch Daniel's relationship unfold—but with Isla. So, her answer was *D*. Horror.

CHAPTER ♥ 26

Emma had texted Isla that her perfect match wasn't Parker (obviously) but someone else, in their grade. Saturday morning, Isla had called her and grudgingly heard her out.

"Forget Parker Clark. I know who your match should be," Emma told her. She was lying on her bed, with Winston fanned out next to her. Winston was chewing noisily on her hair.

"I'm listening," Isla said.

"He's cute with great hair. He's smart, too, and can help you with your homework. He's kind of arrogant."

Erg. Emma wanted to puke, giving all those compliments about Daniel. (Even the arrogant part was a compliment, because she knew Isla would like that.) And she also wanted to puke over the end result: matching him with Isla.

"A fourth grader?" Isla sighed. "Is this a sure thing? Because everyone is waiting to see my boyfriend. Fine. Who is it?"

"Daniel Dunne," Emma said.

"I have no clue who that is," Isla said.

"The guy who was at the frozen yogurt place yesterday," Emma said. "The one your friends thought was your new boyfriend, anyway. They called him cute. He's kind of a catch."

"Oh, the new boy?" Isla asked.

"Yes. He's new," Emma said. "Which means that he has no embarrassing stories about him. Unlike Parker Clark, who used to eat his boogers in preschool."

"Ew, I forgot about that," Isla said. "Hmm. Okay, well, what's so special about this Daniel guy that I should go out with him?"

Isla was as arrogant as Daniel. They had that in common.

"He's smart. He always gets Webber's Winners right," Emma grumbled. "So he gets the best class job each day."

"That's the best you've got?" Isla asked.

"He's from California," Emma said. "And he's met a lot of celebrities."

"Really?" That got Isla's attention.

"Yeah, like Jake LaDrake even." Emma sighed.

"Really. Wow. Okay, I'm in. Hey, if he knows Jake LaDrake, maybe he can get Jake to come here. You can dance and sing with him. The real him. Since you've been practicing." Isla cracked herself up.

Erg.

Emma rolled over on the bed. Winston stopped chewing on her hair and started coughing.

"So, how does this work? Does Daniel text me and ask me out?" Isla asked. "Is that what happens?"

Emma thought about it.

"Should he bring flowers to school on Monday and ask me out in front of everyone? Can you make that happen? We have some zinnias in our garden—can you come over and pick them and give them to Daniel to bring to me?"

"Kak!" Winston coughed. "Khak! Khhhak! Shnuuuurk!"

Winston coughed up a hairball.

"I agree, Winston," Emma mumbled to her cat. "This whole thing makes me want to puke, too." Winston promptly began chewing on her hair again.

"Fine," Emma sighed to Isla. "I'll make it happen. Someone else is clicking in. I gotta go."

Emma hung up, cleaned up Winston's gak, and called Claire.

"Well. Isla and Daniel have been matched," Emma said.

"Well," Claire said. "Congratulations? Sorry? I'm not sure what to say."

"I guess both. I saved EmMatchmaking. But I still need cheering up." Emma's phone beeped again. "Hang on, it's Isla. Probably with requests for more romantic plans for her and Daniel. Hang on."

"Change of plans," Isla said. "Tell Daniel to meet us at the mall. As soon as possible."

"Us?" Emma asked.

"For one thing, you need to be there when Daniel asks me out," Isla said. "To make sure nothing goes wrong this time. For another . . . just meet me at the food court in a half hour."

Before Emma could protest, Isla had hung up. The phone switched back to Claire.

"Great," Emma said. "Isla is making me go to the mall right now so Daniel can ask her out. Then she'll probably make him buy her jewelry and make a cute Build-a-Pet with a romantic heart inside that says I LOVE YOU, ISLA."

"Emma, you sound a little bitter," Claire said.

Emma felt a little bitter. How did she get herself into this mess? How did she get Daniel into this?

"Hey, want to go to the mall?" Emma asked. "I don't want to do this alone."

"I don't want to be alone either," Claire said. Then she let out a sigh.

"Claire, are you okay?" Emma asked.

"Well," Claire said. "Kevin hasn't been texting me much."

Oh. Uh-oh.

"Emma, I don't think he wants to be my boyfriend anymore," Claire said, then sniffed.

Emma Emmets had proved she could matchmake. But now she realized something.

She didn't know what to do about heartbreak.

CHAPTER 🏹 27

The food court was at the very top of the mall. Emma and her dad rode the glass elevator up to the third floor together.

"Thanks for driving me," Emma said, giving her dad a kiss.

"Please thank Claire's mother for chaperoning," her father said. "And saving me from the torture of the mall."

Emma hopped out of the elevator and heard her name called out.

"Hi, Emma!" Rosemeen, Annie, and Leah were sitting on stools at a tall table in the food court with Claire. Emma turned to wave to Claire's mom, who was hovering nearby to chaperone.

Claire was eating a cinnamon bun oozing with white icing; Rosemeen, a sugar cookie with purple frosting; Annie and Leah were sharing a container of soft pretzel nuggets. Emma, however, wasn't hungry. Her stomach felt twisty-sick.

"So, here's the story," Emma said, sitting down.

She told them the almost-but-not-quite-complete saga of Isla and Daniel.

"I can't believe you made a match for Isla Cruz," Rosemeen said. "Impressive!"

"This *is* unexpected," Leah said softly. "For some reason, I thought *you* and Daniel would be more of a match."

Claire and Emma looked at each other but didn't say anything.

"Emma's superpower knows," Annie said. "So we should just trust it."

"Well, it's almost time. Daniel and Isla are going to meet in front of the pretzel place," Emma said. "Then Daniel will ask her out. Then they'll live happily ever after."

"There's Isla!" Rosemeen said. "Wow, she looks great, as always."

Isla said good-bye to her mother and then walked toward them, wearing a white lace dress, a wide brown belt, and boots. Her hair hung in loose waves.

Emma had to admit she looked really nice.

"Hi, Isla!" Rosemeen waved to her. Isla came over.

"Excuse me, I need to talk to Emma," Isla said. She pulled Emma off to the side.

"So I decided no audience," Isla said. "We can save that for Monday at school, when Daniel brings me flowers and makes his public declaration of love. Based on what happened with Parker, I think it should be just me and Daniel when he first asks me, in case he screws it up. And you."

"And me?" Emma said. "Why should I be there?"

"To take pictures of our first moments as a couple," Isla said. "For publicity. Plus, in case I need you for anything."

"And there's Daniel," Emma said.

Daniel was coming up the escalator toward the food court. He was wearing a green plaid button-down shirt and baggy charcoal-gray shorts. He looked really cute. And he was carrying a small bag with a bow around it.

Isla took a deep breath. Emma realized that Isla was actually nervous.

"Go tell your friends to wait around the corner," Isla said. "I'll stand here so you can hide around the corner until I say it's time for pictures."

Nervous . . . yet still bossy.

"I look cute, right?" Isla smiled, smoothing down her dress.

And still arrogant.

Emma hurried over and stood around the corner from Daniel and Isla. She leaned against the wall. This was going to be painful, listening to Daniel ask Isla out.

"Hi," Isla said. "I'm Isla. Obviously."

"Hey," Daniel said. "I'm Daniel. I think we met by the frozen yogurt place? With Emma?"

There was an awkward silence. Emma realized

this match was going to be painfully awkward, too.

"So. Do you have something for me?" Isla asked flirtingly. She reached over and plucked the paper bag from Daniel's hands.

"Actually, that's—" Daniel was interrupted.

"Swedish Fish!" Isla said. "What's with all the Swedish Fish? They must be really popular lately."

Emma heard the bag being crumpled. Then awkward silence.

"Don't you have something to ask me?" Isla asked.

"I guess. Have you seen Emma?" Daniel asked her. "I have to ask her something."

"That can wait," Isla said impatiently. "Fine, I'll do the asking. Daniel, will you be my boyfriend?"

Emma heard silence.

"I said, '*Daniel, will you be my boyfriend?*'" Isla asked again.

More silence.

Then Emma got a text from Isla.

IslaCruz: ??? !!!

Emma popped out from behind the corner.

"Oh, awesome! Emma's here!" Daniel looked flustered. "I need to talk to you."

Isla looked furious. Emma went over to her and whispered, "He's probably nervous. You're intimidating him with your beauty. Let me talk to him."

Isla looked appeased.

"Okay, go advise your client," Isla said. "I'll get a lemon-lime ICEE. But hurry up."

Daniel and Emma were left alone.

"What just happened?" Daniel asked.

"Isla asked *you* out," Emma said. "What, did you freeze or something? Couldn't remember the simple words: 'Will you go out with me?'"

"Of course I can remember that," Daniel shot back. "You're talking to the Southern California regional geography-bee champion who remembers every single capital in Europe."

"Then why couldn't you say it? Six easy words: 'Will you go out with me?'"

"Will. You. Go. Out. With. Me?" Daniel said. "There."

"Now just say that to Isla, and everything will go as planned," Emma said.

"Why would I say that to Isla?" Daniel asked.

"Because you're supposed to become her boyfriend?" Emma said. "Her perfect match? To save EmMatchmaking! And don't try to hide it, I saw you smiling when you agreed to do it."

Daniel's mouth fell open.

"Isla thinks I'm going to ask her out?" Daniel asked. "Won't she get mad when I ask you out then?"

"Ask *me* out?" Emma shriek-squealed. "Wait, you're asking me out?"

"Isn't that what I'm supposed to do?" Daniel looked even more confused than Emma did.

Wha? Huh? Emma thought back on the conversation they'd had. She realized she had never specifically worked out the details. She'd just assumed

Daniel had been thinking of being matchmade with Isla.

Somehow Daniel thought he was supposed to ask Emma out? Did he think Emma was matchmaking him with *her*? They were going to be—*gasp*—boyfriend and girlfriend?

Emma thought back. She remembered that Daniel had smiled when they came up with the plan. He'd been smiling because he was going to ask EMMA out?

Emma couldn't help it. She broke into a smile. Whoa. Daniel had been happy about asking her out?

"Uh, yeah." Daniel looked really confused. "You said you needed to save your EmMatchmaking thing because Isla and Parker was an epic fail. So you and I were going to be . . . uh . . . were going to date."

"Okay, wait. How would you and me . . . um, dating"—Emma blushed just thinking about it—"help EmMatchmaking?"

"A hot brilliant new kid like me asks out a girl? The matchmaker finds the perfect match . . . for herself! That's great buzz!" Daniel said. "And then nobody would listen to this Isla girl when she tried to say EmMatchmaking stunk."

"You don't realize it, but Isla's the most popular girl in fourth grade," Emma said. "She can make or break me. You and me dating wouldn't help that."

Emma thought about the brown M&M incident

and shuddered. That had pretty much destroyed her whole kindergarten. She did not want fourth grade destroyed.

"So," Emma continued, "that's why I needed *you* to ask Isla out."

"Wait. Wait, wait, wait. You wanted me to ask *Isla* out?" Daniel said. "Not *you*?"

"Well, yeah," Emma said. "Well, wait, not really—"

But she didn't get a chance to explain. Daniel continued in disbelief.

"You want me to go out with her?" Daniel said, shaking his head. "You're *matchmaking me with Isla*?"

Emma wanted to explain that she hadn't really . . . that she had gotten confused . . . that she wanted . . . she couldn't . . .

"Glak!" was all that came out of Emma's mouth.

"This is messed up," Daniel muttered. "I kind of thought *you* liked me. Obviously I was wrong, since you're fixing me up with someone else."

"No, it's—"

"If you liked me, you wouldn't fix me up with someone else," Daniel repeated.

Emma closed her mouth. There really wasn't anything else to say.

Isla came bouncing up, holding a pretzel and an ICEE.

"That was the longest line ever!" she said. Then she turned to Daniel and held out the pretzel. "You like cinnamon, right? There aren't any raisins in it. I know you hate raisins."

Daniel looked at Emma.

"Yeah," he said.

Emma wished there was a quiz she could take:

QUIZ: *What Do You Do When Your Crush Who You Thought Likes Someone Else Likes YOU but You're Supposed to Match- make Them and If You Don't There Will Be TROUBLE?*

Emma hadn't known he liked cinnamon. She was impressed. Isla had done her homework.

"I got a preview copy of the new Slick Ice snow- boarding video game, want to play it? I have a game room in my house," Isla said.

"Seriously? That hasn't even come out yet," Dan- iel said. "I love that series."

"I know." Isla smiled. Daniel smiled back.

Seriously. Could Isla make this any more painful for Emma? No. No. She could not.

"I heard you met Jake LaDrake once," Isla said to Daniel. "That's so cool!"

"Yeah," Daniel said.

"Emma loves Jake," Isla said. "He's giving a con- cert tonight, only a few hours away from here. Did you know that?"

Scratch what Emma said before. Isla *could* make it more painful.

"See that store over there? I'm going to be a fashion model for them for a fall festival." Isla posed. Show-off.

"Cool," Daniel said.

"It's the Happy Frogs Fall Festival, where Emma is going to have her matchmaking booth. Isn't Emma a great matchmaker?"

These words, coming from Isla Cruz, should have made Emma feel happy.

Emma looked at Isla. Then she looked at Daniel. They were both smiling. At each other. *They* obviously felt happy.

Maybe she *was* a great matchmaker. So great, she'd outmatched herself.

"So, don't you have a question to ask me?" Isla said to Daniel.

"I guess I do," he said. "Isla, want to go out?"

CHAPTER ❤ 28

"You okay?" Claire whispered as they rode down the escalator together. Emma didn't even turn around to see Isla and Daniel walk off toward the department store that Isla was going to model for. (Okay, fine. Maybe Emma did turn around and that's how she knew that's where they were headed.) Isla was probably going to show Daniel all the fancy-cute outfits she was going to look amazing in at the Fall Festival.

"Swell," Emma grumbled.

"Let's go meet the girls," Claire said. "Oh, wait—ooh! I got a text from Kevin!"

Well, at least someone had good news.

"Kevin's here at the mall!" Claire squealed. "I told him I'd be here and he came!"

Emma scanned. "I think I see him. In the blue jacket. One floor below your mother."

"It's Kevin!" Claire said. Then suddenly her voice changed. "Wait. What if he came to tell me bad news? What if he's breaking up with me?"

"I'll be on standby," Emma said. Then her phone beeped. "Actually, I guess I'll be with Rosemeen, Annie, Leah, and—oh, great—Isla and her mother."

She was resigned to an endlessly depressing day as she and Claire went to another escalator that took them down to the first floor, where Kevin and the other girls would be.

"What if he doesn't like me anymore?" Claire gripped the escalator rail. "What if I did something wrong?"

"Are you hyperventilating? Do you want to talk to your mom?" Emma worried. She looked higher up the escalator, where Claire's mom was following them.

"No, I'm okay! I'm okay!" Claire said. "I need to get this over with. I see Kevin. He's walking toward us. With someone! With who? Is that his new girlfriend?"

"Claire, you're losing it," Emma said, squinting and seeing a tall person in a cardigan and a giant mom-purse. "That's a lady. It's probably his mother."

"He brought his mother to break up with me?" Claire wailed. "What's he going to do, introduce me to his mother and then dump me? Or did he bring his mother so that she can tell me that we're over?!"

"He brought his mother because we're in fourth grade and still can't be in the mall by ourselves," Emma said.

"Oh." Claire stopped and giggled. "Duh."

Emma hoped everything would be okay with Claire and Kevin. This would be a bad day if Claire and Kevin broke up. Actually, Emma wasn't really sure how people broke up. Also, would someone break up when their mother was standing with them? It was all very confusing.

"Well, good luck with everything," Emma said. She watched as Claire walked over to Kevin. Kevin seemed to introduce Claire to his mom, and then the mom moved off to the side to let them talk. Kevin talked. Claire talked. Emma realized she should give them some privacy, so she turned away. Also, she couldn't read their lips from that far away. So.

Emma waited for the other girls. She wondered why Isla was still hanging out with everyone else. Shouldn't she have skipped off into the sunset with Daniel?

Isla and Daniel. Bleh.

ISLA + DANIEL CELEBRITY
MASH-UP NAME:

Isel?

DanLa?

Dansla?

Isniel?

Daniel and Isla, sitting in a tree . . .

Crawwk. Emma made a noise that sounded a lot like Winston with a hairball. If Daniel saw her now, he would definitely think she was going to puke.

Wait. If Daniel were here, he'd be looking at Isla, not her. Sigh.

Emma tried to take her mind off it by looking in the windows of nearby stores. One of the shirts in a window had a picture of two puppies on it and said BFFs!

BFFs, like her and Claire. Emma realized that she shouldn't be grumping about Daniel and Isla, when her own BFF could be having a crushing crush situation. Right now, Claire could be going through a dramatically sad breakup and Emma should be focusing on being there for her. Yes! Emma would! She would be a better friend! She would be the best friend she could be!!!

Emma smiled and then heard her name. There were her new friends coming toward her. Annie, Rosemeen, and Leah were heading her way! (With Isla.) She would be the best new friend she could be, too! (Except to Isla. She'd done enough for that girl already.)

"Where's Claire?" Rosemeen asked.

Emma tilted her head toward Claire and Kevin, talking by the electronic gadget store.

"Aw, that's so sweet," Annie said. "A mall date."

Emma hoped so. The girls waited while Isla's mother went to talk to Claire's mother.

"That is so sweet," Isla agreed. "You know what else is sweet? Daniel. It was so romantic when he asked me out, wasn't it, Emma?" Isla asked. "He brought me Swedish Fish. It was so sad he had to leave right away."

"Mmmbl," Emma said.

"Look, Emma took pictures of us," Isla said, letting them pass her phone around.

"You're such a cute couple!" Annie said.

They *were* a cute couple, Emma had to agree. Em-Matchmaking did result in cute couples. Isla's cell phone beeped, and she checked it.

"And now, Emma, it's time to go to . . ."—Isla paused dramatically—"the department store! The one I'm modeling for at the Fall Festival."

Really? Did they really have to go with her? Emma raised an eyebrow at the other girls, but they seemed surprisingly excited about it, too. They must have been sucked up into Isla's popularity and brainwashed by her shiny black hair. Rosemeen, she would have expected. But Annie and Leah were practically jumping up and down.

Fine. This was really testing her "being a good friend" thing. She texted Claire to meet them at the department store and followed Isla off through the mall.

CHAPTER 29

"You girls stay together in this area, and I'll be right over there," Isla's mother said. "Until it's time."

"Time for what?" Emma asked.

"Time for us to . . . go to another area," Isla said brightly. "Anyway, let's look for cute clothes for the Fall Festival. I have a discount card if anyone wants to use it. They gave it to me because I'm a model."

"This is cool," Annie said. "I could wear this to the Fall Festival." She held up a T-shirt that had garden gnomes frolicking all over it.

"Ha! 'Hanging with my Gnomies,'" Leah read the words on it. "Hilarious."

"For the Fall Festival?" Isla said. "Fashion *don't*! You need to look fabulous! Or at least cute! You'll be going with boys! Don't you want to impress them?"

"It's funny," Annie protested, but she put the shirt down.

"Oh, I like this!" Leah picked up a T-shirt with a unicorn on it.

"Dorky!" Isla rolled her eyes.

"Adorkable," Emma corrected her.

"Look! I could wear the shirt with this," Leah picked up a headband that had a plastic unicorn horn sticking out of the front. "Look, I'm a unicorn!"

She started galloping around the store. Annie laughed and picked up the gnome T-shirt. Then she gnome-walked around after Leah.

"Oh. My. Gosh. I hope nobody from the store sees me with them," Isla sneer-groaned. "They might reconsider my fashion-model sensibilities."

"What do you think of this?" Rosemeen held up a striped scarf.

"LOVE!" Isla squealed. "So cute!"

Emma looked at Isla and Rosemeen. Isla was smiling at Rosemeen with approval. Rosemeen was beaming.

Just then Claire came walking in. Emma rushed up to her.

"Are you okay?" Emma asked her. "What happened?

"First, Kevin said he liked me," Claire said. "But then he said he didn't like everyone teasing him about having a girlfriend. He said it happened so quickly. He feels pressured, like he's supposed to hang out with me all the time or be romantic and stuff."

"Whoa," Emma said. "I'm so sorry."

"No! It's okay!" Claire was . . . smiling? "He was worried he'd mess it up because he likes me!" Claire *was* smiling. "It was good! I said we could slow down."

"A slow-mance." Emma nodded. "That's good. And better than a no-mance."

"A slow-mance is better for me, anyway," Claire said. They both smiled.

"You don't have to rush a crush," Emma agreed.

"Claire! You're back!" Annie and Leah ran up to them. "Everything okay?"

"Everything is great!" Claire said.

"Where's 'I'm a Fashion Model' with her store discount?" Annie asked, holding the gnomes T-shirt. "I'm buying this for the Fall Festival whether she likes it or not. Henry doesn't care if I'm super stylish. And he appreciates my sense of humor."

"Yeah, he likes you the way you are," Claire agreed. "Leah, same with Otto. I bet he'd love your unicorn horn."

QUIZ: Which Animal Best Describes
       Your Crush?

Dog: Loyal, like your best friend

Porcupine: Prickly, hard to get close to

Lion: Likes to be king of the jungle

Turtle: Shy

Koala: Cute and cuddly

Cheetah: Always on the move and hard
    to catch up with

Boa constrictor: Clingy and smothering

"Definitely," Leah said. "I can't buy anything today, though."

"I'll take a picture with my phone and send it to you," Emma said. "You can show him your fierce unicorn look that can take down his and Marshall's zombies."

Leah posed like a fierce unicorn, and they all laughed.

"Now I'll send it to Otto," Emma said, just as Isla looked over and called out to them.

"Don't show that to her boyfriend!" Isla asked. "She'll scare him off!"

"You know," Leah said to Emma. "Otto's not really my boyfriend. I know you EmMatchmade us and everything, so I hope it doesn't hurt your feelings. It's more like me and Otto—and Marshall—are really good friends."

"That's cool. EmMatchmaking isn't just about finding boyfriends and girlfriends," Emma blurted out.

"It's not?" Leah asked.

No, Emma realized. It wasn't. It was more about making matches that . . . made people happier. Slowmances! Friendships! Whatever!

"Leah," Isla called out. "Seriously, take off that unicorn thingy. We have got to get you a makeover for the Fall Festival! You too, Annie!"

Annie wrinkled her nose. "I don't want a makeover. Makeup is annoying."

"Ooh, can you make me look like a unicorn?" Leah asked. "Really glittery? Maybe white face paint and sparkly—"

"Yeesh," Isla said, throwing up her hands. "You two are so dorky!"

"Thanks!" Leah said.

"How did you ever get those two girls matched up?" Isla asked Emma.

"Easily," Emma blurted out. "I found boys who appreciate them just the way they are." She almost added: "On the first try. Without any rejection."

"Rosemeen." Isla turned to a more receptive audience. "Let's go find cute dresses for the Fall Festival."

"Sure!" Rosemeen squealed and happily followed Isla to the dresses.

"I think you made a perfect match," Claire said.

"Isla and Daniel?" Emma sighed.

"No, I meant those two," Claire said, pointing to Isla and Rosemeen. "Didn't you say before that Rosemeen should be friends with Isla?"

"Yeah." Emma straightened up. "I did."

"Also, those two," Claire said. "Leah and Annie. They weren't even friends until you fixed them up with Otto and Henry, who knew each other. Remember how Leah was so shy, she didn't have any friends? Now look at her."

Annie was laughing as Leah chased her around wearing the unicorn horn.

"All thanks to EmMatchmaking!" Claire said.

Yeah. Huh. Emma thought about it. EmMatch-making had done some great things, she had to admit. Things she hadn't been expecting.

Before school started, Emma had wanted to make a name for herself in fourth grade. A real name, not an embarrassing nickname.

And she had done that.

Emma had wanted to help make fourth grade happier. And EmMatchmaking had done that. She was so lost in that happy thought, she didn't notice that the girls had all come over and were looking at her, grinning.

"What?" Emma asked, suspicious.

"It's time," Isla said. "Come with me."

Emma was about to protest, but Claire nudged her forward. Emma followed Isla toward the checkout desk and then behind the checkout desk (weird) and through a door.

"Um, I think this is for people who work here," Emma said, looking around at the boxes and hangers and a sign that said CUSTOMERS ARE ALWAYS RIGHT!

"Like me." A tall woman in a black dress walked up to them. "Isla, darling, our favorite Fall Fest model. How's your mother?"

"Hello, Louise. My mom's lovely. She's right outside shopping, as always," Isla answered.

"Just the way we like it." The woman gave a little laugh. "Follow me down through this door, girls. And be very quiet so we don't disturb the photo shoot."

The photo shoot? Oh, erg. Emma realized that Isla must be taking her to a fashion shoot for the Fall Festival. Why did Emma have to watch? Why would she even care? Was Isla showing off? Or did Isla seriously believe that she was giving Emma a treat by "allowing" her to watch her model? But then why were Claire and Leah and Annie all smiling so much about—

Emma never finished that thought. Because the door opened and they walked into a room full of people. And in the center was a photographer and some very bright lights, and at the center of the bright lights was Jake.

Jake LaDrake.

CHAPTER  30

a.k.a.
The Very Best Moment
of Emma Emmets's Entire Life

Jake LaDrake.

Standing across the room, in the very room that Emma Emmets was standing in at that very moment, was *the* Jake LaDrake. Emma's Jake LaDrake. Live! Moving! Not made of cardboard!

"Surprise!" Isla whispered.

Emma couldn't respond. She was frozen solid, her mouth gaping. Then she clamped her mouth shut so Jake wouldn't see her gawking like a fish. Then she grinned.

This must be the universe's way of paying her back for bringing happiness to everyone! And for sacrificing her own feelings for Isla! And now Isla had brought her . . .

☺ JAKE LaDRAKE!!!!!!!

"Jake," Emma whispered. "It's really him."

Jake LaDrake with his blond, ruffly, perfect hair. His signature green leather jacket and skinny jeans.

His piercing blue eyes, which at the moment were focused lovingly on the posters he was signing so that each one was special for every fan.

BUT those eyes could, at any moment, look up and see . . .

EMMA!!

"Jake is signing posters for our stores as he passes through on his tour," the Department Store Lady explained. "We knew our favorite tween fashion model, Isla, would want to see him. And please don't forget to remind your mother that our fall designwear collection goes on sale tomorrow, dear."

"Whoa," Emma whispered to Isla. "Thanks for bringing *me*."

"Well," Isla said, "I know you're obsessed with him."

Awww! Could it be? Isla Cruz secretly had a heart of gold?

"And you did just matchmake me," Isla said.

Wow! Could it be? Isla Cruz was appreciative?

"Plus, all my close friends are at the fourth-grade lacrosse game, so they couldn't come," Isla said. "And I didn't want to come by myself and look like a loser."

That made more sense. Eee! Whatever! Emma was glad she had made a match for Isla and was on her good side and that all her own friends weren't lacrosse phenoms. She was here watching JAKE LaDRAKE!! JAKE! JAKE LaDRAKE!!!

HE WAS SO CUTE!

"He is really adorbs." Isla sighed. "Let's get closer."

Now that she was in Jake's presence, it seemed Isla no longer thought he was "so over."

The girls inched up closer. And closer.

"Jake," a photographer said. "Smile! This picture will appear on our store website."

"Sure!" Jake LaDrake said.

"He spoke!" Emma and Isla whisper-squealed and clutched each other with joy.

"Don't forget to buy my new perfume, Awake by Jake LaDrake, to awaken your senses with a fresh citrus floral scent!" Jake said, holding up a pink bottle and spritzing it into the air.

What a day. It had gone from absolutely horrible to the best day of Emma's life. Emma was looking at Jake LaDrake!

And Jake LaDrake was looking at her!

Wait—WHAT? Emma blinked. Was she dreaming? No, Jake LaDrake was really, truly looking right at her! And he was opening his mouth to—could it be true?—SPEAK TO HER!

WHAT WAS SUPPOSED TO HAPPEN NEXT:

1) Jake would say: "There she is! The girl of my dreams! The girl I've been waiting for!" And he would break into song: "I'm your perfect match, the perfect match for you!"

2) Jake would leap over the table, get down on one knee, and propose to her.

3) They would get married and JEMMA would live happily ever after. (Jake + Emma! So cute, right?)

WHAT DID HAPPEN NEXT:

1) Jake said: "Who are those girls?" Emma and Isla squealed. He wanted to see them! They practically knocked each other over racing up to Jake's table. "Hi!" Emma said. "I'm your number one fan. I have a Cardboard Jake in my room and your notebook and your stickers and your napkins and your—"

2) Jake got them kicked out of the room. Not even kidding.

As Emma babbled about her Jake pencils, Jake turned to the bodyguard standing next to him and rolled his eyes.

"Girls, you're going to have to leave," the bodyguard growled.

"But I'm Jake's biggest fan," Emma said.

"She really is," Isla said. "She kisses your poster and stuff. I've seen her do it."

"Can't we just get a picture? An autograph?"

Emma's protests were interrupted by the Department Store Lady.

"Looks like it's time to go, girls," she said. "I was just made aware that Jake requested no young people today."

"But—" Emma swiveled her head to make a plea to Jake. Jake?! Didn't he realize that Emma was his soul mate? His perfect match? His future wife and mother of his two adorable children?!!!!

And Jake looked away. As Emma walked away, she heard Jake complain: "Seriously, I asked for no kids. I'm gonna have to deal with a thousand of them screaming at the show tonight. Just a few hours without any crazy girls, that's all I asked—"

Emma couldn't hear the rest. But Emma didn't want to.

3) Jake LaDrake broke Emma's heart.

"Don't forget to buy Jake's new perfume, Awake by Jake LaDrake, coming soon exclusively to our stores!" the Department Store Lady told them as she kicked them out of the room.

QUIZ: Can You Pick Yourself Up from a Heartbreak?

* Are you resilient? You can bounce back from disappointment.
* Are you persistent? You don't give up—especially on yourself.

* Are you optimistic? You can look at the bright side of a situation.
* Are you purposeful? You have goals beyond just a boyfriend.
* Are you supported? You have family and friends to comfort you, cheer you up, and get your confidence back!

CHAPTER 💘 31

It was the big day! The Fall Festival!

Emma was wearing a red shirt with a pink heart on it that she'd purchased with Isla's discount. It was perfect for EmMatchmaking! The green HAPPY FROGS FESTIVAL VOLUNTEER badge clashed but looked official.

"Do you think I'm ready for my booth, Winston?" Emma finished putting up her ponytail and looked at her cat on the bed.

Winston looked up from his furious scratching-fest. He was using Cardboard Jake as a scratching post, and this time Emma didn't scold him for it.

"Jake, do you—" Emma started to ask Cardboard Jake LaDrake out of habit. "Wait, I'm not getting your advice anymore."

Cardboard Jake's face was now decorated in graffiti (pink mustache, green drool, blacked-out eyeballs) courtesy of Emma, Claire, and a pack of permanent markers.

Emma had been sad about Jake. Very sad. She had spent the entire evening after the mall fiasco sobbing into her pillow. (She had used the remainder of her Jake LaDrake napkins to blow her nose.) She pulled her Jake posters off the wall and recapped the horrible scene on the phone with Claire.

But when she woke up the next day, she fortunately had other things to worry about—more important than Jake LaDrake. Emma had been planning what to do in her EmMatchmaking booth.

She'd watched her successful matches and thought about what had worked. She'd also watched Isla and Daniel. Just for research purposes, of course. They had walked to class together. Emma had heard Isla's friends squeal when Daniel walked by. Isla had written ISLA+DANIEL all over her notebooks. Other than that, Emma hadn't seen them together much. Which was probably a good thing.

Emma hadn't spoken to Daniel since the mall. Which was probably also a good thing. Probably. Wait, she had spoken to him. She had said: "HA! I win!" Because Emma had finally been Webber's Winner. Being (the best ever) line leader had taken her mind off her pain just a little bit.

"Knock, knock!" Quinn's voice called out.

"Come—" Emma didn't get a chance to say "in" before Quinn burst into the room (which led Winston to burst out).

"Cupid is here! I'm ready for EmMatchmaking!" Quinn said. She was! She was wearing a red leotard, pink tutu, and white fairy wings. She was carrying a bow and arrow that Leah had cleverly made out of foam pool noodles and duct tape.

"Hi, Q-pid!" Emma grinned. "You are going to be the cutest advertising ever."

Her booth was going to rock. Claire had made an EmMatchmaking booth sign. Annie had blown up red and pink balloons that were floating around inside Emma's mom's van at the moment. Rosemeen had bought bags of heart-shaped candy with sayings on them to put in a little bowl.

Emma packed up her tote bag. Last night, she'd had an idea. She had printed out copies of the quizzes she'd made up over the course of EmMatchmaking. She'd give them to people when they came to her booth. Emma was even thinking about putting them online.

Or even cooler, she could write a book! *Emma Emmets, Playground Matchmaker*. Hehe. That would be awesome.

When Emma was ready, she met her family downstairs for the walk to school. Quinn skipped the whole way there, chattering with their parents, but Emma was quiet and nervous until she walked through the playground gates. A giant sign read

☀ WELCOME ☀
TO THE HAPPY FROGS FALL FESTIVAL!

It looked way different from recess!

Sure, the swings and the teeter-totter were there, but they were surrounded by tents and booths! Emma and her family walked past people setting up for the beanbag toss, karaoke stage, arts and crafts booth, cakewalk, face painting, temporary tattoos, potato sack race, and leapfrog.

Leapfrog! Emma would be pointing that out to Annie and Henry for sure!

It smelled so good. Hot dogs were cooking, popcorn was popping, snow cones were . . . snow coning.

And then Emma looked up. The top of the jungle gym had a bunch of red and pink balloons attached to it, blowing in the wind. Red and pink streamers had been wrapped around the top deck. And a big sign was attached to it.

EM·MATCHMAKER – ❶ ticket

Eeee! There was no way anyone could miss it.

"I'm impressed," Emma's dad said. He admired one of the signs down at the bottom of the jungle gym.

☛ EM·MATCHMAKING!
For CRUSHES or NEW FRIENDS
and for FUN

"Focus on the *F*s," her dad said. "Fun and *friends*."

"Dad," Emma said. "Come on. Didn't you have a little crush on anyone when you were my age?"

"Well," Dad said. "There was a girl in fifth grade

with the cutest freckles. I stared at her from afar, but she never spoke to me."

"Well, if EmMatchmaking had been there to help, I bet she would have spoken to you," Emma said, grinning.

"You know what? That would've been nice." Her dad smiled.

"Oh, I'm so jealous," Mom teased.

"I only have eyes for you," Dad said back.

"Icky squicky!" Quinn said. "Stop being gross. We have serious work to do!"

Quinn was going to walk—well, probably twirl and hop—around the festival with her own sign:

Visit the Playground Matchmaker!
TOP OF THE JUNGLE GYM!

EmMatchmaking was scheduled to be open for the first shift, from ten to noon, of the festival. And now, those two hours were about to begin! Emma walked across the bridge and climbed the platform steps to the very top of the jungle gym, to EmMatchmaking HQ.

"Hello!"

Emma was slightly startled to see a lady at the top of HQ. She was wearing a neon green shirt with HAPPY FROGS FALL FESTIVAL VOLUNTEER on it.

"I'm here to help you out with your crowd control," the lady said. Crowd control? Emma just hoped somebody would show up! She smiled at Emma, then frowned as she looked over the edge. "My, we're up a little high now, aren't we?"

"You can see the whole playground from here," Emma said. "Even my house a little bit."

Emma set up the folders with her quizzes in them. She went up to the telescope and peered through it. She swiveled it around, scoping out the whole playground in its festival glory. Emma remembered the first time she'd looked through the telescope on the first day of school. Who knew it would become her HQ?

"I'm here! I'm here!" Claire came up, panting. She was carrying a large covered bowl. Emma could hear the candy hearts bumping around inside it. "Wow, this is so cool! Emma, are you so excited!?"

Excited! Nervous! Excited! Nervous!

"Five minutes until the festival opens," the Volunteer Lady said.

"HelLO!" someone called out. Isla popped up and squeezed onto the small deck with them. "Emma, I'm here for you to express your gratitude to me."

"You mean you're here to express *your* gratitude to our matchmaker for helping support our cause?" the Volunteer Lady said.

Heh.

"Uh, yes." Isla swiveled her head. "I didn't see you there."

"It's okay." Emma laughed. "Thanks, Isla, for setting this up. It looks great up here."

"You're welcome," Isla said. She went over and peered through the telescope. "Oh, there he is! I've been looking for him. Seriously, I wish Daniel would just get a phone so I could text him like a normal boy-friend. Sometimes I really think he's hiding from me."

Emma did not have a response to that. She knew she should feel bad about it, but she didn't.

"Daniel hides from me, Jake LaDrake hides from you," Isla gave a bitter laugh.

"Technically, Jake LaDrake hid from you, too," Emma said. "So that's *two* boys hiding from you."

"Ha, ha," Isla said. "Maybe next year you should have a comedy booth instead. At least you're laughing and not crying over Jake LaDrake. Jake Heartbreak."

"I only cried for one day," Emma said proudly.

"He's so over anyway," Isla said. "Jake LaFake. Jake My-Perfume-Gives-People-a-Headache. Jake Mistake."

Emma was cracking up.

"You know, you're really funny when you're not being mean," Emma said. "You should use your pow-ers for good, not evil."

"Isla!" Rosemeen's head popped up from the lower deck. "The people from the store have your outfit ready to model!"

"Laters!" Isla said. Then she paused. "Hey, Rose-meen, you should come up and be Emma's first cus-tomer! Rosemeen needs to find her perfect match already!"

Rosemeen suddenly got a panicky look on her face. She shook her head no.

"Okay," Emma said. "But if I'm going to use my skills, I have to do this in privacy with just Rosemeen and my assistant, Claire. My superpower talent doesn't work if someone else is around."

Isla disappeared down the jungle gym. But not before taking three candy hearts.

"One per customer!" Volunteer Lady called after her, to no avail.

Rosemeen looked nervous. "Emma, promise not to tell anyone. I'm not allowed to have a boyfriend. My parents say I can't until later."

"Okay. Totally no problem." Emma shrugged.

"Really? You don't think it's babyish?"

"I'm here to make fourth grade happier," Emma said. "Not make parents mad."

"Cool, thanks." Rosemeen looked very relieved. "What do I tell Isla?"

"If she's a real friend, she'll be fine with the truth."

Emma and Rosemeen turned around. Volunteer Lady had said that.

"It's true," Claire agreed.

"Claire would know, because she's a true friend," Emma said.

"Awwww!" Claire reached over and gave Emma a hug.

"But, Rosemeen, you also can tell Isla that there *is* no perfect match for you here," Emma said.

"EmMatchmaker's superpowers detected nothing. I sense ten years before a boyfriend for you."

Rosemeen gasped. "Ten?!"

"Maybe eight," Emma said.

Emma considered Rosemeen an EmMatchmaking success anyway. She'd made a match with Rosemeen and the friend she always wanted: Isla.

"Looks like they're letting people in," Volunteer Lady said.

Emma went to the telescope and peeked. She looked down and saw Rosemeen pop out of the red twisty slide. She tilted the telescope and yes! The Fall Festival was open! She moved the telescope around. Yup, people were starting to enter and buy tickets. Emma smiled as she saw Quinn bopping around with her sign, their parents close behind her. She watched people heading over to different booths, checking things out, and then . . .

A girl stopped in front of the jungle gym and started walking across the bridge . . .

PLAYGROUND MATCHMAKER was officially ready to go!

A line quickly formed around the bottom of the jungle gym. And it stayed that way.

CHAPTER 💘 32

"Don't forget to visit one of our most popular booths!" the voice over the loudspeaker boomed out. "The Playground Matchmaker, with Emma Emmets!"

"They just announced your name over the whole playground!" Claire squealed.

"They did!" Emma jumped up and down! Then stopped, because jumping up and down on top of the jungle gym made it shake like an earthquake. "I'm popular! I'm a popular booth! Eeee!"

Two hours of EmMatchmaking flew by! Students of all ages told Emma about their crushes, their likes, their dislikes. Emma took notes, made plans, and even made some matches on the spot. Emma had climbed down from her perch only twice to match some kids who couldn't climb to the top of the jungle gym. The time flew by!

And then it was noon.

"Time to close up," Volunteer Lady said. "Em-Matchmaking was a hit."

Whew! Emma was exhausted! And happy! And exhausted!

"Almost all of your quizzes are gone." Claire clapped her hands happily. "They were genius."

"Thank you," Emma said, bowing. Yep. The Em-Matchmaking booth had been a wild success.

"You young ladies were wonderful," Volunteer Lady said, peeking through the telescope. "Er, before you go, do you have any instincts about a certain teacher in this school? His name is Mr. Webber—"

Eee! She had a crush on Emma's teacher!

"Um, I know him, but I think that's out of my range," Emma stammered. "But here. Take a quiz: 'Is Your Crush Right for You?'"

"Thank you," Volunteer Lady said.

Emma noted the name on her name tag, though. EmMatchmaking her teacher? Emma felt like anything was possible today! Maybe if she ran into Mr. Webber later . . .

"Are you going to meet Kevin?" Emma asked Claire.

"Later," Claire said. "He's with his friends right now. First, what do you want to do?!"

"Snow cones! Fake tattoos! Ring toss!" Emma said. "Everything!"

Emma texted her parents to tell them she was done. Then Claire and Emma climbed down to the lower deck. Claire went down the yellow slide. Emma went down the red twisty slide. Whooosh!

Emma whooshed a little too fast. She flew out of the tunnel and landed in the mulch. Thud! Then, pfteh! She spit out a wood chip. She remembered the time she'd had a faceful of mulch chips—when Annie first told her about her match with Henry! Where it had all begun.

"Emma!" Quinn came running up to them. "I made lots of people come to your jungle gym! And I also got face painted. I'm SpiderQuinn!"

"I see that." Emma grinned. Quinn's entire face was now a Spiderman mask, which looked cute and a little insane with her tutu and fairy wings.

"Your friend Leah got her face painted, too," Quinn said. "She's a unicorn!"

"May I get a snow cone?" Emma asked her parents. "And one for Claire for working so hard on EmMatchmaking?"

"Yes, but I need to buy more tickets," Mom answered. "Meet me at the snow cone booth in five minutes. Quinn, you can come with me."

"I need to get tickets from my mom, too," Claire said. "I want to win a stuffed animal. I'll be right back."

Emma walked around the Happy Frogs Fall Festival, checking things out. It all looked different from down here than it had in her view through the telescope.

It all sounded different, too.

"AGGGGGH!!!"

A shriek-wail was coming from behind the curtains on the stage that stood where the foursquare usually was.

"That sounds like Isla," Emma said to herself. Emma went around to the backstage area. Isla was there, standing in front of a mirror.

"But we told you that you were the 'sleepover' fashion model," a woman with a badge from the department store was telling Isla.

Isla turned around and Emma gasp-laughed. Isla's usually sleek black hair had been transformed into total bedhead, sticking up in all directions.

"I'll go get your pajamas and you'll be ready to go," the woman said.

"Pajamas?" Isla wailed. "I have to wear pajamas in the fashion show? I'll look like a big derp! The derpiest derp ever!"

Emma snort-giggled. Then she turned to sneak away.

"I see you, Emma Emmets," Isla said. "I see you in my mirror, laughing at me."

"I'm not—" Emma giggle-snorted. "Okay, I am. Hey, I came to tell you that EmMatchmaking was a big success. The Happy Frogs told me that."

"Fantastic," Isla said, putting her hands on her hips. "I'm glad your booth was great. Because your matchmaking of me with Daniel stinks."

Emma stopped giggle-snorting.

"He is so annoying. He doesn't have a cell phone, so he can't text me cute things like Leah and Otto do," Isla said. "He doesn't walk me to classes like Henry and Annie. He laughed at me when I suggested a wedding like Kevin and Claire. He's never written me a poem. He's never given me any cute presents. He didn't even win me a stuffed animal or buy me a cotton candy or anything today!"

"Oh," Emma said. "Sorry about that."

"You know who's going to be sorry?" Isla growled. "Daniel. I'm breaking up with him. No, wait. You break up with him for me."

"What?" Emma asked.

"You're the matchmaker. Now you can be the match-breaker," Isla said. "Go tell him I'm dumping him. NOW."

The store woman came back. "Here are your PJs!" She held up a neon green onesie. With feet.

"You have got to be kidding. I have to wear *footie pajamas?*" Isla wailed.

"With smiling frogs on them!" the lady said. "Aren't they sweet? We were thinking you could frog-jump down the catwalk."

"Noooo!" Isla wailed. "Get someone else. Make that girl over there be your model. Her name's Emma! Emma Emmets, get over here!"

Eeps!

"I . . . gotta go talk to Daniel for you. Remember?" Emma said. And Emma fled as she heard the lady telling Isla: "If you have to go potty, there's a flap in the back. . . ."

Okay! Well! Emma's head was spinning. What should she do? Should she go talk to Daniel? Wasn't it Isla's job to break up with him? Yes, yes it was.

Emma decided to get a snow cone instead.

Then, as if it were a romantic movie, guess who she saw in the snow cone line?

Daniel. He was wearing a blue T-shirt that said MR. HOLLYWOOD, shorts, and his skater shoes. His brown hair spiked up a little bit in the front.

Emma planned to leave before he spotted her. But he was looking so cute, it was distracting.

Plus, she really, really wanted a snow cone.

"Hey!" Daniel spotted her. "Emma!"

Emma went over to him.

"So, is your EmMatchmaking booth over?" Daniel asked.

"Yup," Emma said. Emma debated if she should tell him something else was over:

Isla - Daniel

"Yes!" Daniel pumped his fist. "So I'm done, right?"

"Done with what?" Emma was confused.

"With Isla?" Daniel said. "The festival is here. The booth is done. I did what I needed to do. The show-mance can be over?"

"I'm totally confused," Emma said. "What's a show-mance?"

"That's what they call it in Hollywood," Daniel said. "A fake romance just for show business? Like when an actor and actress want publicity for a movie or something, so they pretend to go out?"

"Seriously, that happens?" Emma was surprised.

"A show-mance? A faux-mance?" Daniel said.

"Yeah, that happens. All the time. Just like this one."

"Still confused," Emma said.

"I was supposed to go out with Isla because you guys needed to make EmMatchmaking look good. Isla and I were a show-mance," Daniel said. "Emma Emmets, Playground Match*Faker*."

"Wait, that wasn't really what it was," Emma interjected. But Daniel kept talking.

"And we went out. You guys had your booth thing," Daniel said. "Now we can break up."

"Wait. You really don't like Isla?" Emma asked.

"Are you kidding? Isla is driving me crazy," Daniel muttered. "She's always looking for me and bugging me to get a phone so she can text me and tell me what to do."

"Don't worry about it. She told me to tell you that you're broken up," Emma said.

"You better not be kidding me. Are you kidding me?!" Daniel said. "Really? I thought she'd want some loud, dramatic breakup, where she'd tell me I'm not good enough for her in front of all her friends or something."

"There's probably still time for that, if you want," Emma said. "She's over there."

"No way, Jose," Daniel said. "Hide me."

Daniel was now next in line for the snow cones.

"This is awesome news. Hey, want a celebration snow cone?" Daniel asked her.

"Sure," Emma said. "Cherry."

"Cherry's the best," Daniel agreed. "Well, really blue is, but my mom gets mad when I have it because my lips turn blue for days."

"Same!" Emma grinned. As Daniel bought two cherry snow cones, Emma got a text from Isla.

IslaCruz: Did u find Daniel? Is he crying?
Is this the worst day of his life?

"Should I tell her you're crying?" Emma asked Daniel.

"Crying with happiness," Daniel said. "Here's your snow cone."

"Thanks," Emma said, taking it. "So is it weird you had a girlfriend and now you don't?"

"I've had tons of girlfriends and then not," Daniel shrugged. "At my old school, the girls were always like, 'You're my boyfriend,' and then the next day someone else would be like, 'She doesn't like you anymore.' Over and over."

"Weird," Emma said. She looked intently at her snow cone. "Have you ever had a *real* girlfriend? Someone you really liked?"

Emma waited for his response. Emma felt that little teeny feeling she sometimes got from her superpower. The one that said she had a crush on him. And maybe he had a crush on her. And Isla had dumped him, so Emma wouldn't be a Match *Taker*.

IS HE A FRIEND . . . *or Something More?*

Emma had seen this quiz-chart in her magazine. Would Daniel be:

(A) *A budding boyfriend*

(B) *Just a buddy*

"I never had a real girlfriend," Daniel said. Then he paused. "And I don't want one right now. I don't want any more girls in my life. Good-bye, good riddance."

Or would he be:

(C) *A butthead*

The answer was *C*.

"What's your problem with girls?" Emma was insulted.

"This week has been torture city! Isla and her friends following me everywhere, people making kissy noises at me, going *ooooh*! Who needs that? I'm done with girls! I'm never talking to a girl again."

Well. That was that. Emma's crush was *crushed*.

"Never," Daniel repeated.

"Um. You just talked to me." Emma couldn't resist pointing that out. "So you did just talk to a girl."

"Well, not anymore," Daniel said. "I'm done talking to girls."

"You're still talking to me," Emma said.

"AUUUGGGGH," Daniel growled.

"Still talking!" Emma said.

Daniel slammed his mouth shut. Then he grinned. Then he crossed his eyes and made a funny face at her. Then he walked away—but first he raised his snow cone to her.

"Cheers!" Emma couldn't help but grin as she raised her snow cone back in a toast. So. Oh well. Maybe Emma was better off this way, too.

She would just have to look for her next Jake LaDrake—a not-Jake celebrity who really did want to marry a fan. Or at least give them an autograph at the mall.

Emma could just picture it: Emma and New Jake would walk through the festival, eating cherry snow cones and getting matching fake tattoos.

"Do you know who that is?" people would say, pointing and screaming and probably fainting. "And he's with his perfect match, our very own Emma Emmets!"

Emma stopped suddenly, snapping herself out of her daydream. She had realized that her "new" Jake LaDrake looked exactly like . . .

Not a celebrity.

A real fourth (almost third) grader.

Daniel Dunne.

She couldn't help it! She wasn't thinking of a new celebrity Jake replacement anymore.

She was thinking of Daniel.

As if things weren't weird enough, Emma heard her name.

"Emma Emmets! She's the matchmaker," Emma heard someone whisper.

As Emma walked past the teeter-totter face-paint booth, she heard her name again. As she walked by the fake-tattoo booth by the monkey bars, someone else called out her name. Then a girl stopped her at the zip line to ask if Emma could still make her a match.

Emma felt like a celebrity! She didn't even need to be walking with Jake LaDrake. SHE was practically the celebrity. Maybe someday there would be a Cardboard Emma Emmets!

"Emma!" This time it was Quinn calling her name. Emma walked over to where her sister was standing. "I'm matchmaking, too! Come see!"

Quinn was standing next to a tall girl Emma recognized from lunch. She was holding a leash with a golden-red retriever puppy.

"Hi, your dog is so cute," Emma said.

"My new friend's name is Jane, and her dog is Ginny Weasley," Quinn said. "Ginny Weasley is going to be Winston's new girlfriend."

"Um, Quinn, Winston is a cat," Emma said.

"That's okay," Quinn cooed, leaning down and patting the dog. "They'll be a perfect match. They're both chubby gingers."

Emma and the girl started cracking up.

"Hey, aren't you in fourth grade?" Emma asked her.

"Yeah, I'm new," the girl said. "I'm Jane."

"I'm—" Emma started to talk, but her voice was drowned out by the loudspeaker.

"Announcing the Happy Frogs signature event: the leapfrog competition," the announcer said. "All participants, please line up at the edge of the swings with your partner."

Emma noticed Jane perk up for a second.

"Are you going to do leapfrog?" Emma asked. "Do you want us to hold your dog for you?"

"I would, but I . . . I don't have a partner," the girl said.

Emma looked at the girl. She looked hard, looking into the girl's soul to find out what she really, really needed. She noticed that Ginny Weasley's collar had a familiar pattern with red and gold lions. She also noticed the girl was tall, with long legs. . . .

Emma sent off a quick text.

A few seconds later, Annie and Henry and Leah and Otto walked up. And Marshall.

"Emma," Annie said. "Leapfrog for Happy Frogs! This is how it all started for me and Henry."

Annie and Henry gazed happily at each other.

"Guys, this is Jane," Emma said. Then she lowered her voice, so only Jane could hear. "See the shorter guy? He'd be a good leapfrog partner for you."

Just then, Ginny Weasley the dog started jumping toward Marshall, trying to play.

"Sorry, she thinks you're going to throw the stick to play with her," Emma said, pulling on the leash.

"That's not a stick, that's my wizard wand," Marshall said, waving it in the air.

"Oh, my dog knows that." Jane smiled. "Her name's Ginny Weasley. She knows it's a wizard wand. She just thinks it's hers."

Marshall looked at Jane with respect. Jane looked at Marshall and smiled.

Emma looked at both of them and *felt it*. Her superpower, her talent, her gift. Emma Emmets, Playground Matchmaker, making fourth grade happier!

"Oh, sadness," Claire said. "Kevin's still stuck in line at the basketball shooting booth."

"Claire," Emma said. "Want to be my leapfrog partner?"

"Definitely!" Claire said.

Emma went with her friends to the area behind the swings, where people were lining up for leapfrog.

"Last call to line up for leapfrog!" the announcer announced.

Annie and Henry. Leah and Otto. Jane and Marshall. Hey, Violet and Aiden were there. And Kendall and Nathan. And Claudia and Adam.

Isla and Rosemeen were there, too. Isla was practicing jumping over Rosemeen. Rosemeen cowered while Isla kept kneeing her in the back. Poor Rosemeen. Heh.

Then Emma saw Daniel. He spotted her, too. He grinned and pointed right at Emma.

"Do you want to be Daniel's partner instead?" Claire asked her.

"Oh, no. I'm your partner." Emma smiled. "Besides,

he's not asking me to be his partner. He's telling me he's going to beat me."

She noticed Daniel had partnered with a boy who competed in gymnastics. A wise choice.

"Hey, Emma! I bet you didn't know that in India leapfrog is called leap *horse*?" Daniel yelled.

"He's trying to intimidate me," Emma muttered to Claire. "Don't let him shake your nerves."

Then she raised her voice.

"I bet you didn't know that in France, leapfrog is leap *sheep*!" Emma yelled back. Ha! Take that!

"You two are weird." Claire shook her head.

Emma gave Daniel her most intimidating look.

"Are you okay?" he yelled to her. "You look like you're going to puke."

"It's ON, Daniel Dunne!" she yelled to him. Oh, it was on.

Claire got into crouching-frog position. Emma got into leaping-over-frog position.

"Go, Emma Emmets!" a voice yelled from high in the air. Emma looked up to see Quinn on the top of the jungle gym, cheering her on and waving a used, but still very sparkly, sign.

EM·MATCHMAKING!
For **CRUSHES** or **NEW FRIENDS**
and for **FUN**!

Emma Emmets, Playground Matchmaker

Matchmakery Word Search

```
S  Y  H  S  U  L  B
S  Q  U  E  A  L  Y
T  E  U  Z  Q  L  P
U  X  M  I  G  Y  P
N  C  N  N  S  T  A
N  I  I  W  R  H  H
E  T  C  O  O  L  Y
D  E  E  B  T  W  Y
A  D  I  Z  Z  Y  P
```

Blushy	Shy
Squealy	Squishy
Happy	Nice
Stunned	Tingly
Excited	Dizzy
Cool	

WORD SCRAMBLE!

Qualities to Look for in a CRUSH

. . . .

oftnceind

nynuf

eicn

dkin

eptrcseluf

oesthn

gcrian

nseeoiratcd

WORD SCRAMBLE ANSWERS

. . . .

confident

funny

nice

kind

respectful

honest

caring

considerate

ACKNOWLEDGMENTS

Caroline Donofrio, editor and inspiration for all
   things Emma Emmets **✚** *Ben Schrank*, president and
   publisher and king of the playground
✚ *Vivian Kirklin*, managing editor
✚ *Rebecca Kilman*, editorial assistant
✚ *Emily Osborne*, cover designer
✚ *Maia Rigas*, interior designer

= T E A M   R A Z O R B I L L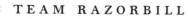

Mel Berger, literary agent extraordinaire
✚ William LoTurco, agent assistant

= TEAM WILLIAM MORRIS ENDEAVOR

And my
   David DeVillers, husband ♡
   Quinn DeVillers, daughter ♡
   Jack DeVillers, son ♡
   Robin Rozines, mom ♡
   Jennifer Roy, twin sister and author of
      other fab books ♡
   Adam Roy, nephew ♡
   The Twitterhood of the Butt-Lifting Pajants ♡